KUN LUN

Liisa Cay Pasila
KUN LUN

To my father Master Manu,
who passed on September 3rd 2010
at the age of 88 in my arms
with a smile on his face – the way he had always
wanted to leave this world.

ACKNOWLEDGEMENTS

While writing this book, I came to realize how much I am loved. My husband Jamie and my daughter Leena made great sacrifices to ensure the necessary time and peace for me to complete the project I had started many years ago, but which was always interrupted by other obligations. Without you two Kun Lun would still lie unfinished in my drawer. I am immensely blessed to have you in my life.

I also thank my little dog Mimi, who lay at my feet, night after night and brought Ni-hau into the book.

My deepest gratitude to my teacher and friend His Eminence Prof. Samdhong Rinpoché for showing me there is more to this world than meets the eye.

Thank you J.M.L. Dandia, Hanne Lahdenperä, Tytti, Dwight Porter, Manolo-Padre, Pedro Vidal, Nina Monasterio, Timo Leskinen, Tarja Vähätiitto and Subtropic for friendship, encouragement and advice.

A special thanks to my publisher Thor-Fredric Karlsson, my graphic designers Steven Stansbury and Soile Kesäkoski, and my literary agent Marianne Gunn O'Connor.

And thank you Tara, Saint Francis of Assisi and all my Spiritual Sponsors for enlightening my path by sharing your Ray of Light.

Liisa Cay Pasila

Look to this day,
For it is life,
The very life of life.
In its brief course lie all
The realities and verities of existence,
The bliss of growth,
The splendor of action,
The glory of power –
For yesterday is but a dream,
And tomorrow is only a vision,
But today, well lived,
Makes every yesterday a dream of happiness
And every tomorrow a vision of hope.

Look well, therefore, to this day.

Sanskrit proverb

MASTER LI WANG stepped into the beautiful garden of his house. The Year of the Tiger had begun two moons earlier, and the cherry tree was in full blossom. A flock of sparrows was singing around the pink flowers, resting their tiny wings. They had flown in from the small holes especially designed to welcome them. The sun was shining through the glass roof, which Master Li had decorated with paintings by his own hand. The little birds chirped merrily when they found the heap of seeds he had placed in a large marble bowl.

The garden was Master Li Wang's most cherished work of art and he knew it well; he had spent twenty years creating and perfecting it. It was constructed inside his house, at the heart of the large mansion he had inherited from his parents. A wooden door with a heavy lock separated it from the rest of the house.

He breathed in the soft perfume of the flowers and bowed in deep emotion.

It was time to leave.

He closed his eyes but the image of the garden stayed unaltered in his mind. He could have painted it from memory and neither one single plant, nor one small pebble, or any of the detailed carvings in the wooden bridge over the pond, would be missing. He smiled and gently touched the leaves of a huge square bamboo tree, which was reflecting its silhouette on the surface of the water.

The garden silently shared his mixed feelings of sorrow and excitement.

As he bent down to caress the smooth head of a goldfish, the crystal clear water of the pond reflected an image of a slim middle-aged man with a thin white beard and a long ash-gray braid. The straight line of his nose, his thin lips, and his ivory pale skin, revealed he was a nobleman and from distinguished origin.

Master Li Wang was a renowned artist, but his heart was heavy with years of loneliness and a fame that left him indifferent. He longed for the peace his garden so naturally possessed. He sat down on a flat rock without opening his eyes. The wide sleeves of his cobalt blue silk gown were hanging flat on both sides and the golden dragon embroidery on his back was shining in the sun.

The garden slowly faded away, changed shape, and was transformed into the image of his beautiful wife TaiTai, who had been his inspiration for creating the garden. She smiled at him and he felt loved. Suddenly everything started to tremble and TaiTai's loving expression turned into terror and desperation. He felt her hand cling to his sleeve before she fell into the deep crack, which the Great Earthquake tore between them. He could hear her hopeless screams as he watched, in horror and with powerless outstretched arms, how she was buried under the rubble.

Master Li opened his eyes to stop the painful memories from pouring into his mind, but the pond had changed into a dusty bottom of a crack, the fatal tomb of his beloved. In a few tragic moments the cruel Quake had buried his joy of living and left him alone in the world. To maintain his love alive and TaiTai's beauty always present, he never remarried. During his endless mourning he built, within the walls of his mansion, a private sanctuary for his beloved.

No one but the sparrows and his servant had ever seen it.

呂 呂

Master Li was brought back to the present by loud, pounding steps. Another image appeared next to his on the surface of the water; a tall, stout man with a sun burnt face, lively brown eyes and a black ponytail, had entered the garden. It was I, Yu, his servant. In the mirror of the pond my smile looked much wider and my lips thicker than they were, but I was as strong and healthy as the image.

Master Li Wang and I seemed to have nothing in common, but we had lived together in perfect harmony since the Great Quake. He was of royal blood and a highly learned man. He spoke many languages and one of his paintings decorated the Imperial Palace. His poems were widely read, and Wan-Li – the 13th Emperor of the Ming Dynasty – had them recited at the Palace during visits from abroad. Some of his works had been sold overseas and translated to other languages. Master was a wise man, so he never got involved in the political affairs of China, though he did not agree with the general belief that the goods brought by foreign merchants were neither needed nor welcome. Mongolian, Japanese and Korean attacks were weakening the powerful Ming Dynasty but, due to Master Li's discretion over state issues, even the enemies of Wan-Li respected him and his art. His education included a three-year retreat in a Buddhist monastery in Beijing, where he had also received the Sword of Honor. He was a talented musician and I loved to sit at his feet when he played the flute. I admired him more than any other man, even more than the Emperor, but I'd never admit that to anyone – I might find myself in a prison cave.

In contrast, my origin was humble. I believed in the Great Tao, though I knew little of my religion. I tried to be honest and hardworking, for I was sure my parents were keeping an eye on me from the secret land only dead ancestors inhabit. I survived the Great Quake, but had no memories of what happened. I was told I had knocked on Master Li's door five days after the Quake, hungry, naked, and unable to utter a word. I knew my name was Tang Chi, but I was mute and had no way of letting others know my name. My Master started to call me Yu.

After the Quake we moved to Guilin, for there was not much left in Shenxi due to the magnitude of the disaster. Besides, Master Li thought Guilin was the most beautiful spot on earth. During the years that followed, he developed a sign language to help me express myself. However, I kept the name he had given me because I felt I had been reborn.

Master Li made me swear I would never show his garden to anyone. He even invented a special sign for it: he put his palms together, crossed the middle fingers and moved them up and down like wings of a little bird. We used the sign only when the garden had to be mentioned in the presence of others, but only we two new what it referred to. He taught me how to read, write and count, so I was able to communicate with the villagers by drawing characters in the air or on my palm with my finger. There are many dialects in China and it is a common way to understand each other, because most dialects were written with same characters. I also learned how to use some of the healing plants of the garden.

Without my Master's kindness I would have died of hunger and cold, or succumbed to the terrible diseases, which had spread out over the

Shenxi province, wiping out entire villages. But most of all I learned to trust and feel safe. Master resolved all problems with calm perfectionism. I sometimes tried to copy his manners, but I was hot-blooded and had no patience.

"Horses ready, Master need more things?" I asked him with our sign language.

He shook his head and returned his gaze back to the pond.

⚜ ⚜

The preparations for our journey had begun years before we left Guilin. They started with Master Li's growing restlessness and with his braid slowly turning gray. His thoughts were no longer in his art; he just sat in silence in the garden with his eyes fixed in the depths of the pond. Over and over again, he kept reading a Sanskrit proverb, which a friend of his had given him long ago. It was a beautiful piece of advice on how to find a better way to live. It was a poem called 'Look to this day'. One day Master called me to his garden and said:

"Yu, an old Chinese man has said that if you want to be happy for one night, get drunk; if you want to be happy for one moon, get married; if you want to be happy for the rest of your life, become a gardener'. I have done all those things, but I am not a happy man. Buddha says that I must let go of all attachments if I wish to be free from sorrow. This Sanskrit poem urges me to find happiness in today, but my heart is in yesterday and tomorrow. I can not rest until I shall be reunited with my long gone wife. I miss her very much."

His eyes lit up when he continued:

"According to an old legend somewhere in the heart of Asia stands a mountain so high that it reaches up to heaven. If you climb up to its peak, you'll be blessed with all you long for. It is the Mountain of Light – the great Kun Lun. Many men have drawn maps to find it or tried to explain how to get there, but the road leading to it is different for every man. I believe that anyone who seeks it shall find it. My wife TaiTai came to me in a dream saying she was waiting for me at Kun Lun. I must leave Guilin and go to her, even if it means I shall never return. You can stay here and take care of my house. If you want to follow me, we will leave next spring."

I listened to Master bewildered, remembering the tales my grandfather used to tell me when I was a child. He had heard stories of men who had found the mysterious mountain on a high plane behind the Himalayas. They had all come back wholly changed. One of them had had a shining golden light around his head, one had reached a peace of mind beyond all understanding, and one was known to levitate after sunset. But many had gone and never returned. My grandfather had said there were seven iron gates on the road to the peak, guarded by man-eating monsters and dragons spitting fire. The horror-stories of what happened to those who attempted to go there had made my grandfather's lips tremble and my teeth chatter.

In spite of my fear I agreed to accompany my Master. It was my duty as his servant. He changed all his possessions for gold, except the house, which he decided to leave under the care of his nephew Jei-ming, who lived on his own in the house next to Master's mansion.

Jei-ming had been my first and best friend when I came to live at Master's house. We were nearly the same age and, in spite of him being short and skinny, he was a worthy opponent in our childhood wrestling matches. Due to his wonderful sense of humor, which was a contrast to Master's seriousness, he was great fun to be with. I was always happy to welcome him at the mansion and he was the only person – apart from Master Li – who had learned my sign language. Though he was a frequent visitor and a trustworthy man, he had never been allowed to see the garden or the secret sign referring to it.

꒦ ꒷

I was getting impatient. Everything was prepared for the journey; three horses were ready in front of the mansion. One was loaded with provisions and two were waiting with empty backs, but Master Li just sat and played with the goldfish.

"Master needs something else?" I repeated with stronger gestures.

"No, the less we carry, the lighter we will travel. We have all we need, the rest will be provided along the way. Please ask my nephew to come in."

I ran to fetch Jei-ming.

When he entered the garden, he stopped with his mouth wide open, startled by the beauty surrounding us.

"Oh! Oh! How… how is this possible?" He staggered. "I have visited you since I… since I was a child and never seen this!"

Then Jei-ming realized that he was to be in charge of the house. He flung his hands across his chest and cried out in anguish:

"I have no means to keep this beauty intact till you come back!"

"Just feed the fish and water the garden. You know I may not return," said Master Li calmly.

"But uncle…!"

"Do not worry about the future, just do every day what you think is best. That is enough. If the garden dies, it has served its purpose."

Then Master asked us to leave and wait for him outside.

I walked backward nodding my head several times as a sign of respect. Before I turned away, I saw him stroke the flat rock he was sitting on and I heard him whisper:

"How difficult it is to part from things you love, even if they tie you to sorrow and pain."

Then he walked out of the mansion and bowed to the statue of Buddha at the front garden. He united his palms on his forehead and prayed:

"Buddha of all times, may your wisdom accompany our journey and guide us to Kun Lun, where I shall be united with my beloved wife."

I looked up to the sky and asked also the great Tao to protect us on the way, just in case his prayers were not heard.

The mansion got smaller and smaller as we advanced, until it slowly disappeared from sight.

RIVER LI, 'the silver ribbon' Master had described in his poems, was winding around the green hills of Guilin. The landscape was incredible; the hills were separated from each other and arose from the flat ground as if the earth had been boiling to form them one by one.

In all the years I had served Master Li I had never been outside Guilin. If he had to travel, I stayed and guarded the mansion in his absence. I was somewhat troubled by the dangers of our journey through the wilderness. I was accustomed to the safety of Guilin, where I had been able to make myself understood with the villagers with sign language. I had gone to the market every day to buy food, and there had been people close by when I needed help during Master's travels.

If something happened to my Master I'd be lost. Nevertheless, I looked forward to the adventure ahead of us, and I was fascinated by the enlightenment Master talked about.

The monsoon season began early that year, but we were warm and dry in our water buffalo-skin tent. There were also many caves and small villages on the way, so we had no difficulty finding food and shelter.

During the first monsoon of our journey Master Li taught me how to listen to the rain. I learned that I was part of something wonderful and became friends with the Tao of Nature.

Master Li's teachings were mostly Buddhist, but he usually explained things to me in terms of Tao, so that I may better understand. I listened to him attentively when he spoke, but things he said were often too complicated to comprehend.

To me everything was Tao, sacred and full of mysterious spirit. I believed every stone, plant and living being was part of some kind of magical Unity of All Things. When Master said that there was nothing permanent in this world and that all things were interdependent, to me it meant that the world was Tao.

When the monsoon ended, we slept on our mattresses under the open sky and Master talked about the stars. I felt an absorbing bond with the sky and imagined myself as a star, floating in space, with millions of other stars in an endless chain of light.

When I got tired of walking, Master trained me

to hug trees. He said that, if we approach a tree with respect and ask to share its power, it would give us energy and strength.

I found it to be so.

With trees, stars, rain, and the sounds of animals at night, I gradually lost my fear of the wilderness. The only animal I was still afraid of was the tiger, though I had heard it never attacks unless wounded or threatened. It was considered good luck to see one and I wished that, if we needed luck, the tiger would pass us by from afar.

⊰ ⊱

One night I woke up to a sharp and insisting bark of a dog. The autumn darkness was almost total. The fire had gone out and clouds covered the moon. I heard horses running away and whistled to wake Master Li, but there was no answer. I whistled louder. The silence and my gloomy thoughts made me jump up and hurry to his mattress.

It was empty.

Fear gripped my throat and I started to make a new fire to see in the darkness. As it lit up, a terrible sight was revealed to me.

My Master was lying in a pool of blood only a few feet from where I was standing. He was still breathing but there was a profound wound on his jaw. I knew that, unless I managed to close it quickly, he would bleed to death.

I poured a generous amount of rose liquor on the wound and thanked Tao for Master's unconsciousness. This must burn like Dragon's breath I thought, and confirmed it with a sip.

I found tiny ginkgo twigs and made little clips from them, closing the cut neatly from both sides. When I finished, the wound stopped bleeding.

I looked around and noticed that his sack lay empty next to him.

The gold!

My first thought had been that some wild animal had attacked Master Li, but quickly understood that we had been robbed. I was transporting half of the gold around my waist, under the robe, so all was not lost.

When I carried Master to his mattress and covered him with a blanket, I noticed a shaggy-looking dog near the fire. It must have scared the bandits off with its sharp barks. I threw a piece of cake on the ground to show my gratitude and the dog swallowed it whole.

All three horses were gone and the last village we had seen was many days behind us. I looked at the sky. A new moon was coming out from behind the clouds. It was an auspicious sign, which relieved my fear of Master Li dying.

When the sun rose the next morning, it found me sitting sleepless and my Master groaning with pain. I whistled softly and he opened his eyes. He made an effort to speak, but I raised my hand to keep him quiet. I knew that if he refrained from speaking, the wound would heal sooner. He tried to smile, but it was too painful.

With our sign language, which he himself had invented and taught me, he said:

"Now we are equals."

We'll never be equals, I thought, shaking my head. Then I made him drink a big cup of rose liquor, which sent him back to the floating state of unconsciousness.

The next day he asked about the horses.

"Gone," I explained with swift gestures.

"The gold?"

"Your part gone – my part here." I showed him the small leather bag on my waist.

"Bandits took everything," I explained. "That dog saved us." I pointed at the hairy creature next to the fire. "I woke up to her barking."

Suddenly I was filled with enormous guilt and threw myself to the ground.

"Oh Master! I failed in my duty and let bandits attack you!"

The intense worry over his health and the relief of seeing him recover, came out with tears.

"I am a bad servant!" I shouted with my hands.

"Shhhhh," he hissed. Then he drew signs on his palm. "If it had not been for you, I might be on my way to a new reincarnation. You have profound sleep because your conscious is clear. What did the bandits leave us?"

I showed him the cooking gear, the flint stone and the food next to the fire.

"Ah, it is not much. Maybe you can find some mushrooms and herbs in the woods," he gestured.

I stood up immediately and noticed the dog was still sitting next to the fire. She was a medium-sized female with a golden brown coat. Her ears and neck were bravely erect and her corner teeth were long and sharp. She reminded me of a wolf. Her eyes were amber and she was staring at me. I stared back at her.

Suddenly she started running towards the woods. Then she stopped a little further away and looked back. I decided to follow her and she ran away.

I found some mushrooms and fruit in the forest and the dog disappeared.

When I returned to the camp and started to make soup, the dog came back carrying a dead rabbit. I looked at it and prayed in silence. I was hungry. While I prayed, she walked to Master Li and, without wavering, dropped the rabbit on the ground. How can a wild dog do what she just did? I thought.

I skinned and cleaned her prey. Then I put it in the soup with the mushrooms and rice and thanked Tao for the miracle. I bowed to the dog with gratitude and gave her the leftovers. She walked around the fire with obvious pride before retiring to the bushes to eat.

From that day on she hunted all the food we

needed. At first Master refused to eat meat – he was a vegetarian, but after several days without food, and when I had nothing else to offer him but a pheasant, he sighed and gestured:

"It makes me sad that such a precious animal must give its life to nourish me. I hope it will not be this way for long."

Then he took the dead pheasant and rocked it in his arms. At the same time he was humming a beautiful melody, which seemed to spring from his heart like a fresh fountain. The air around us was vibrating with a strange wonder. I was so impressed by his act and the compassion he showed for the dead bird, that I was the one who was unable to eat that night.

Master named the dog Ni-hau, which means 'you are good'.

We advanced very slowly. I had made a carrier for the tent, the mattresses, our blankets and the cooking gear, but it was a heavy load to pull – even for me.

Master was still weak, though his wound closed faster than we expected. He gave me instructions to cure the wound with a thick paste made of ginkgo leaves, salt, garlic and mud. I made him a cup of cinnamon tea several times a day and added some ginseng root in it.

⚐ ⚐

Master directed our route following the stars. We walked for one whole moon and arrived at the next village exhausted. Master decided to stay until we had both recovered our strength.

"We are not in a hurry," he said. "And if we were, there would be more reason to slow down."

Soon I was back to my normal strength, and Master's wound healed almost completely, leaving only a purple scar. The ginkgo clips had worked so well, that the cut had closed neatly. And since it was right under the jaw nobody noticed it.

I thought it was very wrong that Master had been attacked and robbed. He was a good man and did not deserve such a fate. When I apologized again for not having protected him from the bandits, he told me a story:

"Two monks from a nearby convent were walking on the beach. Suddenly they heard cries for help and saw a naked woman fighting the waves of the turbulent sea. The elder monk quickly undressed, swam to the woman, and dragged her to safety. Then he put his robe back on and the two monks walked away.

After a long silence, the younger monk asked:

'Tell me brother, how could you do what you just did? You know we are not allowed to neither look at naked women, nor touch them.'

The elder monk replied with a smile:

"Dear brother, she was drowning and crying for help. I went and got her back to the beach. Then I left her there. But you are still carrying her."

Then Master continued:

"What ever happens, happens according to the Law of Karma – the law of Tao. Everything we do is written in the Book of Life. Some past action of mine created a debit in the book. The attack was my opportunity to cancel my debt."

Then he looked at me with a serious expression:

"We are on the road to Kun Lun. We are on the way home. We are all – the entire humanity – on our way to enlightenment. We can see the journey as a wonderful adventure of learning, or curse the inevitable pain we sometimes must go through. The more we complain about things that are not according to our will, the more we suffer. If we shut our eyes to the blessings we have today, we see no light at the end of the tunnel. When we focus on the wonders along the path, we can truly see life as it is: A miracle. But no matter how we live our lives, we will all eventually return to Tao."

I listened with enthusiasm. My heart recognized his words. I had always known that what he was saying was true, but I had been unable to form them into thoughts.

He continued:

"The further along the spiritual path we walk, the more our earth-bound self rebels. It does not want to go home, because spiritual life offers no food for him. 'I-should-have', 'I-could-have' and 'I-wish-I-had' is its language, for it has high expectations for us. But we are allowed to fail those expectations. In fact, we must fail. Failure is necessary for spiritual growth; it strips us of false pride. It provides us with a wonderful opportunity to forgive ourselves for being human. But our earth-bound identity tries very hard to maintain the illusion that we are omnipotent and that we must succeed in everything we do – and be better than others. And it always lives in past or future glories."

He looked at the sack where the Sanskrit poem was.

"Yes, we must look to this day, our own day, and not compare ourselves with others. There are people who are closer to home than we are, and some are still walking behind us on the pebbles we have already trodden. Our earthbound self does not accept the reality of today. It has great plans for our future. When we admit our powerlessness over life and death, it deflates. When we love, it becomes useless."

※ ※

The people at the village were extremely hospitable. They helped renew our provisions and we bought some medicine in case of further adversity. People called us 'pilgrims' and they shared their food and homes without reservations. I became aware of the fact that I was a servant of a pilgrim who was on his way to Kun Lun. That made me a pilgrim too. The thought gave me a sensation of grateful dignity.

Ni-hau followed us faithfully. She had become part of our lives and I was happy to feed her during our stay in the village. It was our turn to give.

One night we met a merchant from Kashmir. His name was Zeenath. Upon hearing we had lost our horses, he offered to sell us his old female yak, assuring that she was well tempered and that she gave good milk. He was on his way to Siam and, since he was convinced the yak would not survive the heat, he wanted to send it back to the Himalayas.

"Himalayas! That is where we are heading," my Master said thrilled. "We are in search of Kun Lun, the Mountain of Wisdom and Enlightenment. Have you ever heard of it?"

The fat, bearded merchant scratched his head and nodded.

"Oh yes, yes I have. I met a strange naked man near Katmandu and he sat with me for a meal. He had not eaten anything for weeks and I couldn't believe he hadn't frozen to death in those heights.

He had no clothes on and no fuel in his stomach."

The merchant burst out laughing and patted his huge round belly.

"I get furious if I miss one meal!"

Then he sat in his thoughts for a while and continued:

"There was something special in his eyes. I'm sure he didn't suffer a bit. He had found peace, he told me so, and I couldn't ask him anything because I felt like a clumsy beast sitting next to him by the fire. He told me he had seen the Light of Kun Lun and attained liberation from suffering."

Master grabbed the merchant's arm with enthusiasm and said:

"I'll buy your yak and take her to Tibet with us, if you sit with me tonight and tell me every detail of that man's story."

In the evening I built a fire and prepared tea for my Master and the rough Kashmiri merchant. They engaged in a busy conversation and my Master's eyes were shining with delight when the merchant assured him that if any man had ever reached enlightenment, it was the naked stranger.

"It's difficult to say though," the merchant said

wiping his bearded mouth with his sleeve. "I've met all kinds of people on my long journeys and most of them are more or less out of their wits. They lie and cheat and make up wild stories just to add a few coins to their thick purse. But that man didn't ask for anything, neither did he have anything to sell. I gave him my gown and, ask anybody who knows me, it's the only time I've given anything free of charge!" the merchant said laughing. "I am a merchant. I make a living from doing business. The man made me feel like a human being, not the cash monger I thought I was. He truly impressed me. He looked like the paintings I've seen of Western Saints, you know, with this golden light on top of his head."

The Kashmiri drew a circle over his head.

"Did he say where he was coming from? Did he give you any indication of where the mountain was?" Master asked excited.

"Oh, indeed he did. What a story! He said that there was a village at the foot of a mountain surrounded by green pastures beyond the Himalayas, on a high, flat plane. A tropical valley in the middle of snowy peaks! It sounded very strange, but

I believed him."

"Yu, did you hear that?" Master turned to me. "It must be the Valley of Comfort!"

I nodded in awe.

"That's the name he used! But there is no mention of any valley by that name," said the merchant and opened a big paper roll. "This is the most recent map I have. I can give it to you at a very reasonable price."

Master studied the map and decided it would help our journey considerably. He bowed to the merchant and said:

"I thank you my friend for this valuable information. Our meeting was most fortunate! Tomorrow we shall continue with renewed spirits."

I heard them bargain over the price of the map and the yak until both of them were satisfied. The Kashmiri laughed out loud and said:

"I'll have some fun tonight with a girl who winked an eye at me this morning. My father always told me to work as if I were to live forever, and to love as if I were to die tomorrow. I take his words very seriously!"

Then he paused and turned to me.

"One more thing…the name of the yak is Ying-kha. She eats a lot, but like that naked saint, she endures anything! Sometimes she gets a little moody with this bitter look on her face, you know." The merchant showed an angry frown and I laughed. "It's because she needs sweets. If you want no trouble, give her some. Sugar calms her down immediately and makes her tame as a baby sheep."

❧ ❧

Encouraged and refreshed we continued our journey.

Ying-kha carried our provisions; we rode the two horses we had bought at the village. Ni-hau was jumping with joy to be part of our adventure.

"Dogs sure know how to show their excitement," I said to Master Li with sign language.

He laughed at Ni-hau's acrobatic vaults and continued:

"Dogs are wonderful animals. They teach us true devotion and they heal our spirits. This brave new friend of ours will keep the bandits away and hunt food if needed. I hope that will not happen, my body is still upset by the dead corpses it had to digest."

Then he turned to me.

"When we love an animal, we give it a sparkle to become human in its next life. If we let a dog love us, our heart grows soft and we become a little more compassionate with ourselves and other living beings. It's a beautiful friendship where both are enriched and blessed."

I liked animals and my Master's words made sense. It was interesting to hear that I might do something to benefit the animal realm. They had so few defenses against the abuse of men.

"The weather is getting cold," he said later that day. "I think it's time I teach you how to keep warm."

We camped in a cave and I made a fire at the entrance. Master asked me to sit cross-legged by his side on the cold rock with my face towards the fire.

"Look at the flames and close your eyes, retaining the image in your mind," he instructed and I obeyed.

"You will see alternating colors. Feel the warm energy of the orange. Concentrate on it and then inhale it."

I took three deep breaths and imagined I was inhaling warm, orange air.

"Let the heat spread out into every corner of your body. When you exhale, visualize the warm orange color come out of your lungs and form a circle around you. Can you see it?"

I nodded.

"Good. Keep breathing. Spread the heat around you, slowly and rhythmically. Not so slowly, let your breathing flow naturally. That's better. Let it fill every extremity of your body, all the way to each and every finger and toe."

After a while he said I could open my eyes. I did not feel any warmer, but he said that practice makes a master.

Then he added:

"The day will come when you have no need for a live fire to keep you warm. You just breathe and you will be warm. We shall practice together. I learned this technique at the Tibetan monastery and it works if you practice it long enough.

Thoughts have great power and we can make miracles happen if we train our minds. But we are repeatedly told by others that we can not do this and we can not do that, so we have no faith in the power we have inside."

I felt privileged to be with my Master. He was wise and kind, and I was learning many things with him.

However, I was sure I knew nothing yet.

WE JOINED A CARAVAN of merchants heading towards the Big City and traveled safe during several moons. The caravan carried carpets, silk, furs, paintings, spices, jewels, and hand-made carvings to the Far West.

They were exciting days for me.

I learned many new things from those button-nosed, white-skinned foreigners and my knowledge of the world increased immensely. I learned that – while we were on the road to Kun Lun – a man called Drake had departed with the intention of sailing around the globe. The Russians were conquering Siberia and a new calendar was about to be introduced in the West, where a terrible plague had wiped out millions of people. I also heard about entire populations of Indians dying of fever in the continent south of the New World, which had been named America.

Master Li listened spellbound to the stories about an Italian artist, who had painted wonders on the walls of churches and chapels in Italy. He had recently died, but those who had seen his works said that no man had ever created anything more beautiful.

There were people from all corners of the world in the caravan. I liked the Spaniards. They were fun and they made me laugh with their jokes, though I needed many explanatory waiving of hands to understand them. Their language was easy and I learned some of it through listening and watching them. I had the sensation that the words they used were already stored in some mysterious hidden corner of my mind. I thought that maybe I had been Spanish in some earlier life.

The Spaniards prayed to a cross and wore necklaces with golden carvings of saints, as did the French, Portuguese and Italians. The Arabs and Persians prayed to Allah and bowed towards Mecca on small carpets, in long, prefect rows. But no matter what the people called their beliefs or gods – Christian, Buddhist, Muslim or Hindu, it became clear to me that the Great Tao was present in all their complicated religious ceremonies.

The music Master Li played with his flute in the evenings gathered admirers around our campfire. We often sat together till past midnight and Master Li explained to me what they talked about. Many celebrations took place in the caravan and they were the highlights of the journey. The Westerners commemorated solemnly the birthday of their God Jesus and we were invited to a succulent dinner.

Soon after their New Year number 1580 began, our Year of the Tiger ended. The Year of the Cat promised less danger for travelers, and we danced and drank wine to rejoice it.

⚎ ⚏

When we reached the Big City, I was excited to see thousands of fires and oil lamps light up the dark horizon. The City was surrounded by a thick, stonewall and it was the colorful and busy center for merchants who came from all over the world to buy and sell their goods. I had never in my life seen so many people and goods in one place. It was full of noises, unpleasant smells, and dirty dust. The agitated traders were shouting aloud, repeatedly praising their goods as the best. The curious crowd wandered around the markets from stand to stand, never seeming to make up their minds. There were spices, swords, pigs, textiles, beggars, camels, jewels, furs, laughter, thieves, food, elephants, slaves, rich men, white men, black men, dirty men, tents, screams and busy bargaining from dawn till dusk.

We bought new clothes and lots of provisions, including some luxury items such as sandalwood incense, Western paper, books, ink and brushes made of camel hair. By then we knew that Ying-kha would not move if we ran out of sweets, so we bought large amounts of halvah-sweets.

The noise and bustle in the Big City was too distressing for Master Li. He decided we would camp outside the city walls – which would have been dangerous without Ni-hau. I was also so accustomed to a quiet life with my Master, that although I had dreamt about seeing it one day, I did not like the Big City.

Leaving it behind was a relief to me, but the noise had taught me to appreciate the peace there was in silence. We traveled through the monsoon season with good speed. When the cold winds of the North started to blow, we arrived at a small timber production valley, which was surrounded by a huge pine forest.

Master decided we should stay there through

the winter moons. Though there was plenty of gold left – living was cheap at the mountains – I got a job cutting down trees, because a cozy log cabin was offered to us as part of the wages. In addition, we did not want to draw attention to Master Li's gold.

I was content with manual work and spending time in the woods. Doing nothing bored me. It gave me the sensation that I was throwing away time.

Ni-hau came with me to the forest and started hunting again. I made some great roasts with her help, but Master preferred rice, vegetables and barley porridge.

I had never seen snow before. When the first snowflakes fell from the sky I stood still and watched. They were like tiny clouds trickling down very slowly. Time seemed to stop when they landed on my face and everything was quiet and peaceful.

I became so skilled in maintaining my body heat that I could even roll naked in the snow without getting cold. It was great fun and Master Li roared with laughter as he watched me.

Something wonderful – yet so painful – happened in that village.

※

There was a young girl living in the house next to ours. She had long red hair down to her thighs, green eyes and small feet. She was beautiful. When the wind played with her hair and snowflakes fell on her eyelashes, she laughed out loud. I felt a joy of living simply watching her movements.

The devotion I felt was a new experience, I had never been in love. I wanted to be near her, massage her small feet, and make better her world. I wanted to follow her wherever she went, protect her from suffering, and be there if she needed something.

Not knowing how to deal with such passion, I started to keep a diary. I filled page after page with descriptions of her clothing, details of her gestures and the shades of copper in her hair. Every smile she gave me was written down.

One day I noticed bruises on her arms and that she limped a little. At night, my notes were full of questions as to what could have happened to cause her such injury.

It did not take long to find out that her name was MiMi San and that she was married to a middle-aged man, who had been beating her for years.

I tried to put on paper the rage and worry I felt, but found it very difficult. My life had been centered on Master Li since I was a child. I had only considered his desires, his thoughts, and what I could do for him. I had never stopped to think about my own emotions very often; I was a friend with my thoughts and a stranger to my feelings.

Master and I got involved in her tragedy the night we heard screaming and shouting from outside. I opened the door and saw the neighbor beating MiMi San with a log.

He was trying to hold her still by pulling her hair and there was blood on her face. She tried to protect her head with her arms, letting out short, sharp screams.

I was well aware that women were men's property by law. Outsiders were not allowed to interfere with the way a husband treated his wife, even if he killed her.

To my relief, Master Li came to the door and said:

"Stay here, I'll go."

I watched him walk towards the neighbor and say something to him. The man let go of MiMi San's hair and she ran home. Master talked with the man for a while and then came back.

When we were inside the house, I asked him with gestures of beating:

"Why he hit her?

"He had seen his wife smile at you. He said she is not allowed to smile at anyone but her husband," Master Li replied.

"What you say to him?" I asked.

"I told him you were a eunuch."

I threw my hands in the air.

"What?!"

"I said that you are a castrated, brain-damaged mute, thus no threat to his property. And that his wife must have smiled at you out of pity." Master giggled.

I did not know what to think. She had been brutally beaten because of me. Moreover, she was married and I had no right to dream of her the way I did, but I did not want her to think that I was less than a man. Then I concluded that the most important thing was her being alive and that the beating had stopped.

"The neighbor will be leaving for the Big City tomorrow. He will not come back until the cherry trees blossom," Master Li added as he sat down and crossed his legs for meditation.

I sat with him and prayed fervently for Tao to protect her during the night.

The brutal neighbor left the next day and MiMi San came to thank us for rescuing her the night before. While curing the cut in her temple, Master Li told MiMi San what he had said to her husband. She laughed to tears.

I was relieved she found out the truth, even if it made no difference to her.

Two sunsets later, I watched her pick flowers in the garden. She walked to me, gently tilted her head and said:

"I know you are mute, but try to explain to me what you think when you stare at me like that."

I showed her the biggest star coming out of the darkening sky.

A satisfied smile appeared on her face. Then she pushed a curl off her face and blushed. With an unexplainable urge I caught her in my arms and pressed my lips against hers. At first she pushed me away, but then her arms wound around my neck. Her caresses made me dizzy and I felt like choking.

She burst out laughing, holding her stomach with both hands, and said:

"You must breathe through your nose when we kiss or you'll die."

Her words threw danger in the air and I instinctively looked around.

"My husband is gone and he will not come back until the cold season is over. Do you like poetry?"

I nodded my head.

"I cannot read, but I have a book of Chinese poetry, which I know by heart. I could recite my favorite poem to you. Would you like to come and visit me?"

I nodded again.

"Tonight?" She asked.

I took her hand and kissed it. She drew it back shyly and put it on my cheek. It was a tiny, cold hand, but her touch was warm and soothing.

That evening, with burning cheeks and a pounding heart, I went to her house and we made love.

Though I was in my thirties, I had hardly any sexual experience. She had been married for over five years and, in spite of her young age and fragile looks, she was a woman who knew how to please a man.

I found overwhelming happiness in her arms.

The next morning, with Master still fast asleep, I crossed the garden back to our cabin. While serving Master's morning tea, he made a short comment:

"She may bring some enlightenment to your life but let no one see you visit her."

I nodded shyly and carried out my household tasks as if nothing had happened, but I heard each bird that burst out singing, and my steps where as light as falling snowflakes.

Working in the forest had made the muscles in my arms and chest grow. I had never thought of myself as a handsome man, but now I looked at my body with new pride. I was like Emperor Wan-Li – potent and powerful.

Every day from then on, when the last snowy

tree-trunk fell tumbling to the ground, I returned to our cabin full of anticipation. After making dinner and feeding the animals, I left the house and crossed the yard to see MiMi.

Our nights were filled with passion – I hardly slept at all – but I was not tired in the morning. MiMi taught me that a man could endure anything if he is loved.

⚎ ⚏

The winter passed quickly and too soon we welcomed the Year of the Dragon. The warming weather filled me with anguish. I knew MiMi's husband was coming back. I wanted to stay and yet knew it was impossible.

Every newborn leaf that appeared in the cherry tree pierced my heart like a dagger.

The April sun was melting snow into crystal clear streams, when the neighbor's galloping horse announced the end of MiMi and me.

The day he arrived, Master Li said to me:

"We shall leave tomorrow. All we can do is pray for her."

That night my imagination drew horrible images of MiMi with her husband and I cried for the first time since the Quake.

At sunrise, when I was loading Ying-kha, I saw her once more. Her tears and her copper hair were shining in the sunlight. She slowly put her palms together on her breast, bowed to me and turned away. I was about to run after her when I felt Master's hand on my shoulder.

"My dear boy, it is her duty to stay. Do not make it any harder on her. A woman cannot leave her husband, no matter what. If she tries to escape, she will be burnt alive. If we took her with us, we would face death also."

I nodded and went inside the house with a heavy heart.

Master asked me to sit down. He took out his flute and said:

"Breathe the music I play to you. Do the same as when you learned to keep warm. Let the sounds of my flute comfort you."

His kindness and the beautiful melodies touched me deeply. But I was sad. I was terribly sad. Tao seemed malicious and unjust. I did not know how to accept such unfairness.

After a while Master Li put the flute in the sack and said:

"Buddha taught a special prayer to relieve suffering. It is very, very powerful. It also helps others who are faced with hardships and abuse.

It is called Metta.

Start with forming in your mind a clear picture of your face. Keep visualizing it and say to that image:

MAY YOU BE WELL
MAY YOU BE HAPPY
MAY YOU BE FREE FROM SUFFERING
AND DANGER.

Repeat the words for a while, looking at your own face."

I did as he asked and he continued:

"Now, form in your mind a clear picture of a person you love. Hold it in your mind and say to that image: May you be well, may you be happy, may you be free from suffering and danger. Repeat the words for a while, looking at the face of your loved one."

I visualized the sweet face of MiMi, sighed, and obeyed.

"For the third round, you may choose the face of any person who is indifferent to you. A shop-keeper, someone you have seen working in the field, – someone who does not arouse any special thoughts or feelings in you. Repeat the prayer, – may you be well, may you be happy, may you be free from suffering and danger. Retain the image and keep praying."

I chose Zeenath, the Kashmiri merchant, for I did not like or dislike him in any special way.

"The fourth and last person to pray for is your enemy, or the person tormenting you in some negative way. Form an image, keep it clear, and pray."

My neighbor seemed to stand right in front of me, but I had no desire to pray for his well-being.

"It is difficult, I know from my own experience," Master Li said reading my mind. "But I assure you that this prayer is extremely beneficial. It works miracles. To end Metta, put all four persons together in one image and repeat the prayer once more to them all. Just remember the words and

choose any four persons any time you are troubled."

With great effort I managed to pray for MiMi's
husband, although it was against all my instincts
and seemed outrageous.

Then we got up and left the village, but my heart
stayed behind.

WE FOUND a crossroads with a northbound road and two almost parallel ones leading west, – which was our direction. Master descended from his horse and I waited for his decision.

He sat on the ground and closed his eyes. After a short meditation he got up, lifted his hand to one of the parallel paths and said:

"That one."

"How do you know which path is the right one?" I drew on my palm.

"We are heading west and there are two roads to choose from. I asked for guidance and listened to the answer. If we ask for help, we receive help," he replied. "Sometimes we just do not like the answer," he added.

"You pray for Tao when you need help and your need is Tao's opportunity to strengthen your faith. Gods dwell in crossroads, because that is where wise men ask for guidance. The path I chose, might not be the quickest, the easiest, or the shortest way, but it does not matter. We can take either way because no man ever makes mistakes. He simply chooses and learns. And his mistakes are his best teachers."

"What do you mean with 'no man ever makes mistakes'?" I gestured. "People make terrible mistakes. Sometimes a life is lost because of someone's error!"

"Nothing in this universe happens against the Law. Not one leaf falls without consent of the Tao. When the time comes for our earthly life to end, it ends – no matter what others do. The only exception is a person who has taken on some unselfish task – something that would greatly benefit his fellow beings – but there's no time left for him to finish the task. That person is often granted extra time in this realm."

"What about those who are murdered? Or those who died in the Quake?"

"We leave this earth when we are done here. Life continues on a spiritual plane, free from the bondage of self. In the spiritual realm we see our past life through the eyes of Love and receive the wisdom of the universe to prepare our next life. We choose our parents and the best possible environment to reincarnate and learn the unlearned lessons."

What he was saying sounded complicated. He added that there was no lasting happiness on earth, that everything was interdependent and in constant change. He called it the Unfolding of Creation.

"Why did we survive the Quake?"

"Because we had not fulfilled our missions yet."

"How do I know what is my mission?"

"Since you are still alive and here with me, your mission for this Year of the Dragon seems to be on the road to Kun Lun. The most important thing in life is to be active. You may choose to walk the eight-fold path taught by Buddha. You may seek to find a God of your understanding, or strive to grow closer to Tao. You may work to make this world a better place. Each person walks his own path with the knowledge and wisdom he has.

When you get confused, rest and ask for help. Sometimes you cannot hear the answer and must rely on your own judgment to continue."

"What if I do evil instead of good?" I asked bewildered.

"There is no good or evil. All things are either beneficial or not beneficial. Those who intentionally cause suffering for their fellow beings are ignorant of the Law of Karma. Someday, somewhere, in another life or life form, they will have to face their actions. Every word, every thought, and every action is recorded in the Book of Life. Remember the bandits? They will face their actions some day. But those who seek, or are willing to seek, the well being of their fellow men, not only benefit themselves. They create more Love in the world. And Love melts the hearts of those who cause suffering."

"I do not want to cause suffering to any living creature. I want to do good...I, I mean things that are beneficial. How can I distinguish when what I do is beneficial or not?"

"By making mistakes."

"Can I avoid making mistakes?"

"Yes. By asking for guidance and then listening to the answer."

"How can I learn to listen?"

"When you pray to Tao, you talk to Tao. When you meditate, you listen. You already know how to relax your body and concentrate on breathing. I will teach you more very soon."

The sun was very bright and the sky was clear when we climbed the first frozen peak. The intense light transformed snow into a shiny blanket, as if millions of diamonds were scattered all around us.

Unaware of the danger, we both stared at the brilliant scenery during several days, until we reached a small community formed by one single family of thirteen members. Our skin was burnt to blisters and our eyes blinded by the sun and snow. We had to spend a whole moon with our eyes covered by black cotton scarves and get a servant to take care of us both.

The first evening, when we had finished our meal, I heard Master say:

"Now that we are both blind, we can both improve our senses and I can learn to listen without words. If you need to say something important, come and draw the characters on my hand, otherwise just talk to me with your thoughts.

I have taught you many things since you knocked on my door, but the pupil is always master's best teacher. You are mute, but I do not speak the language of the people in this village, so to them I am as mute as you are. You talk to animals and they understand you, so maybe you can teach me the language of the heart."

I was too tired and too sad to say anything. The village and the women I had seen when we arrived brought back painful memories.

He heard my sigh and continued:

"I could never have imagined a better teacher than you. Your company has been a blessing to me. It has been a reward much greater than the gift I gave you. You are suffering now and I share your pain. I know only too well how excruciating it is to lose someone you love. For many years, I built a garden to maintain my memories alive. I tried to ease my pain with art, because expressing yourself, even without talent, is like a soothing balm to your wounds. When we can see again, you may use my camel hair brushes and rice paper to paint or write."

His compassion brought tears to my blindfolded eyes. In spite of the intense hurting and longing, I had wonderful memories. Master used to say that it was better to have loved and lost than not having loved at all. When he heard my sobs, he continued.

"Tears are our natural protectors against despair. Like a spring stream, they cleanse our hearts and unburden our minds. Let them do their work. I wish I could cry too, but my well is dry. The day I shall be reunited with TaiTai, the doors of my heart will fling open and life will return to my dead veins.

To talk about pain is difficult because we think no one can understand, but no human being is a stranger to heartaches. A burden shared with others leaves you less to carry alone.

Many men try to drown the unfairness of their world in wine or burn their sorrows with opium, only to find more confusion and a bitter end. The brave, when defeated in a battle against drugs, get up and find a better way to live. They learn how to accept this world as it is.

Acceptance is the key to happiness.

When you are done crying we can do the Metta and light a few candles to help our prayers rise to the sky."

I searched for his hand and drew a sign on his

palm to say I was ready. He patted my hand softly and continued.

"Now that our eyes are blindfolded, we are living in a temporary darkness. In the same way, man lives in a spiritual darkness here on earth. Even though he sees the shape of the world around him, a veil is covering his eyes. He thinks he is alone, separated from Tao and his fellow beings. But it is not so. We all come from the same Source and we are made of the same Essence of Life.

We look up to the sky for something more powerful than us, but that power is already inside us. It is everywhere. Meditation opens our eyes to a new awareness. I shall now teach you the basic steps to lift the veil. Practice will show you more."

All wise men meditated and I was eager to learn. I wanted to be like my Master – full of knowledge and experience!

He explained:

"When we meditate, the invisible channels connecting us with Tao start opening. Fresh winds blow into our minds like clean air when we open a window. Our attitude and outlook on life will change. Tao enters through the channels, which are often blocked by fear. Compassion and peace pour into our minds.

Sometimes this meditation and its purifying effect cause some readjustments in you. Do not fear them. They are a natural consequence of your awakening. You may start to sleep more – or less. Maybe you will find that you start eating less meat. Your body will adjust to the new spiritual condition you will have, as it sees best. Ready?"

I took a deep breath and he continued:

"Sit as comfortably as you can and take three more deep breaths to cleanse your body a little. Relax. Let your limbs grow heavy. Feel their weight. When you know that your body is comfortable and at ease, pay no more attention to it. Breathing has a natural rhythm. No effort is needed to inhale or exhale. Your body knows the task well. Observe calmly how air enters into your lungs and comes out again. Like a tide, it goes in and out, in and out. Thoughts will cross your mind, and your ears hear sounds, but let them flow with the tide. In and out, in and out. Now, start counting them. One breath, two breaths, three, all the way to ten. If you think of something else and forget to count, start all over again."

I could not count to more than three when my thoughts – like arrows, invaded my mind.

"The thoughts, the sounds, the feelings in your body, have no importance to you at this moment. You are safe.

Just observe the air go in and out. It is very simple, – just breathe."

I noticed my breathing slow down and my muscles let go. Soon I lost notion of my body. I did not remember whether I had placed my hands on my knees. Maybe I crossed them? I did not know and could not look. Many thoughts came to my mind, but I did not try to force them go away. When I lost the counts, I just started to count from one again.

Time passed in silence until I heard Masters voice:

"Good, that's all. You can now slowly move your arms and feet and feel your body again."

I saw that my hands were on top of each other on my lap.

I was somewhat disappointed for I had not experienced anything special. Only stupid unimportant thoughts had come to my mind to bother my counting. I drew 'failure' on his palm.

"You are doing well, no reason to worry. This is only the beginning of a lifelong romance with the universe, – your Tao."

Since he was always right, I put my doubts aside and fell asleep to the melodies he played on his flute.

⚌ ⚍

We started meditating together twice a day. Master said it was not advisable to meditate with a full stomach, so we did it before each breakfast and dinner.

As soon as the scarves were removed from our eyes, we climbed the nearby hill to see the sunset. The sky was slowly changing from blue to red, yellow and orange. The moonlight cast a ghostly gray light on the snow and the stars came out one by one. I watched in ecstasy, as if I had never seen the sun go down.

Master pointed out to the horizon and said with a gentle voice:

"You are part of all this, Yu. The stars, the trees,

74

and all living creatures are your equals. You have the right to live in this world and paint it with your own colors. You have the right to walk your own path. You where born from the same source as everything you see around you. There is nothing more important or less important than you, and your spirit holds the same beauty as this sunset. They are both reflections of Tao."

I waived my hand in protest and signaled:

"No, I see wonders around me while I am flawed and ignorant. And Master, meditation bores me. I'm getting nowhere with it."

I bowed my head in shame and heard a thump.

Master Li had fallen on his back. He was clapping his hands and laughing hysterically. I stared at him without knowing what to think of his odd behavior.

Soon he calmed down and said:

"You are learning very fast to get lost so soon! Of course meditation is boring, and of course you are ignorant! How would you learn anything if you knew it all?"

He started to laugh out loud again and applauded amused.

"How can you fill a glass of water if it is full already?"

I got totally confused. Then I noticed that he had called me ignorant. It was one thing to call yourself stupid, but that someone else would! I felt awkward, and my incapacity to understand the glass of water made me feel worse. Then I wondered whether his blindness had affected him in some strange way.

We returned to the house in silence.

During the night I had a dream:

Master Li was standing on a huge rock holding a plaque 'do not follow'. Instead of being written with Chinese characters, it was painted with images of my sign language. Then Master suddenly disappeared and black clouds surrounded me. Somebody gave me a brush and red paint. I started to write a Chinese character on each cloud. As soon as I completed one cloud, it disappeared. When I finished, the sky was bright and silvery blue.

The next morning I described my dream to Master Li.

"A very auspicious and revealing dream," he

said. "It seems you do not have to listen to me so intensely anymore, because the plaque was written in your sign language. Maybe you must start following your own inner guidance. What did you write on the clouds?"

"I don't know. I wrote characters I have never seen, nor do I remember what they looked like."

"Well, whatever you wrote made the clouds go away. You stood under blue skies. It means you will be able to solve some problem soon without my help.

Monsoon was late and for some reason Ying-kha got very difficult to handle. We gave her sweets all day long, but they had no effect on her ill temper. Then we finally found the reason for her irritation and bad mood; she had a thorn stuck in her armpit.

Master removed it, and we finally got a kettle full of milk without her kicking and spilling it on the ground. However, she was clever – as old bitches often are – so she learned a trick; she would not move in the morning after we milked her, unless we gave her sweets.

"We have spoiled her like grandparents spoil

their grandchildren," said Master Li amused.

We agreed on two sweets every morning, one in the evening, and Ying-kha continued to serve us without further trouble.

There was no rain and the draught got severe. We had to change our route and follow rivers, but many of them were dry. During the cold season it had been easy to melt snow and make a cup of tea at any moment of the day.

Ni-hau rescued us once more; she learned to bark at water. Whenever she found a stream, a pond, or simply a small crack in a rock with a few drops of water, she would proudly come and let us know. We learned to distinguish her 'water here'-bark from 'food there'-bark. She amazed us to a point where we both believed she was a goddess in disguise, sent to take care of us.

In spite of the heat and my melancholy, life seemed different. Falling in love had softened my heart. A beautiful landscape filled me with wonder and I appreciated my Master's company more than before. His monologues were a rich world of wisdom and I understood him better than before. We both had lost a loved one. There were long silences between us; nevertheless I had the sensation that we did not cease to communicate with each other. He helped me understand how isolated I had been most of my life due to my muteness and fear of revealing my innermost thoughts and feelings.

⚏ ⚎

"You are very quiet today, no gestures and no characters in the air," he said one night when I was preparing our evening meal.

I felt troubled.

All of a sudden my blood chilled, my feet got weak, and I was unable to move my arms. My ears started to whistle and I had a feeling something terrible was approaching but I did not know what. I instinctively ran to Master for shelter. I could hardly breathe and he got worried.

"Yu, what is it? You do not look well."

I could not explain what was happening. I was paralyzed by fear. I just stood there and stared at him with my arms hanging on both sides.

"Come and sit here, I'll bring you some sugar water. It's the best remedy for anguish."

I grabbed his arm to make him stay close to me. There was sand and wind on my face and a dreadful image came to my mind. It was the Quake. The earth shook violently under my feet and I watched people flee in panic. Thick dust covered my eyes, my nose, and my mouth. Hills and houses were torn apart and a gigantic rock buried my family's cries for help. Earth swallowed my sisters and my brothers. The cruel monster-earth swallowed all life around me.

I fell on my face and wept like a little boy, the same helpless boy whose world had been shattered and who had not wanted to survive. I felt his anguish and his loneliness. The Quake robbed him of his childhood and threw him in the frightening world of adults. He did not understand why and he had nothing to say; no one would understand him.

I felt as if a huge dam had broken and the waters were flowing free.

I knew I could speak.

"You are free my dear boy, it is over." I heard Master say. "You were too young to face it then."

I was burning with desire to say something but,

when I tried to form a word, my tongue refused to obey. Only a groan came out of my throat.

Master lifted his hand in warning.

"Make it easy on yourself," he said. "Do not spoil your joy with asking too much of yourself. You will recover your speech and words will come back to you. You have done very well for one evening. I'll make dinner tonight."

Master Li was famous for many things, but cooking was not one of them.

He decided I should rest after the profound emotional experience of remembering the Quake. While he was preparing the meal, he chatted along and made some praising remarks on my skills in the kitchen. He had a way to make me feel proud of myself, though I did not think I was much of a cook.

He talked about food and heath and gave me a long lecture on healthy living:

"It is very important, that the things we eat please the eye and taste good. When that happens, our body rejoices in digestion and food gives us energy and health. If we eat when we are distressed or filled with negativity, we cannot digest properly.

Then food becomes a burden unable to benefit us.

There are men who punish the flesh with long fasts, convinced that when the body shrinks, the spirit will swell. However, our body is a holy temple. If we nourish it wisely, exercise it daily and let it have enough rest, it will take care of itself without any special effort on our part. It's like a lamp that needs oil to burn.

Live food is very beneficial for us. Sprouts and green vegetables, curd, nuts, mushroom and garlic, are essential in our diet. So are most berries and fruit. Honey, ginseng root, rock salt, spices and herbs are very valuable too. Whole grain rice keeps the stomach clean. Meat makes men aggressive and eating an animal is like eating your own children.

I am very fond of seaweed because it makes me strong and you prepare it in such a delicious way. Since we cannot get it here, I must only imagine eating it – which in reality is almost the same since we nourish ourselves with thoughts too. When you are happy and joyous, so is your body. When you are in distress, the body agonizes. If people knew how much negative thoughts and feelings shorten their lives, they would flee from those poisons like from the pest. Moderation is the best guideline for healthy living. Yin and Yang must be in balance."

He paused for a while and continued:

"I believe peace and joy are the secrets of long life. Meditation gives you both. Fear, doubt, anxiety and desires which really means insisting on having your will done are powerful enemies, which can throw us into utter confusion."

I was not listening very keenly.

I thought about the fact that Master had always treated me as if I was his own son. Maybe his kindness had given me the courage to face what happened during the Quake. Perhaps MiMi had brought out the little boy I had abandoned in the shadows of my mind. Or – could Metta give such an amazing result?

At night I lay awake looking at the starry sky. I thought it would be a pity to go to sleep and waste the happiness I was experiencing. I was grateful to Tao for my liberation and meditated and prayed all night.

In the morning I opened my eyes and pronounced two syllables:

"Mi Mi."

Master Li looked at me, raised his eyebrows, and said:

"I must cook more often!"

Then he laughed at his own joke and I laughed with him. He stroked his beard in thoughts, nodded several times, and said:

"Metta is truly powerful and you have loved enough to break your isolation. It will not take long to have a real conversation with you. I am tired of my monologues and will welcome listening to you. You have a lot to say after keeping silent for over twenty years!"

He kept nodding his head, contented.

"Oh yes, it is time for me to listen to you now. It has not been easy to hear no other echo but my own voice. You have been a good listener. With your help I will also become one now."

I could not wait. I would gladly give him everything I had.

Along the curves and changing horizons of our path, I slowly recovered my speech. Ni-hau and Ying-kha were stunned to hear me call their names instead of whistling to them.

It was staggering to speak out my thoughts, though I never learned to do it very fast. The short silence between thinking and expressing myself with gestures remained.

IT hAD SNOWED for half a moon in Katmandu, when we arrived at a peaceful-looking town in a valley at the foot of the majestic Himalayas.

There was a monastery in the center square with a beautiful statue of Buddha. It was made of pure gold. I thought how tempting it must be for bandits, but we were later told that the monks had created a protecting circle around it by meditation and prayer, and that nobody had ever tried to steal it.

Upon our arrival, the Abbott of the monastery received us in person. He invited us to stay over the winter and offered us some awful tasting yak-butter tea. We sat down with him and Master Li translated what he and I said. Later I learned enough to have a simple conversation without his help.

Master introduced himself:

"My name is Li Wang, I am originally from Shenxi. I paint and write poetry. I strive to follow the eight-folded path of Buddha, but I sympathize and learn from any wise man whose teachings I find enlightening. After losing my wife in the Great Earthquake, I moved to Guilin with a little orphan boy who has served me ever since. This is Yu."

I bowed and said to the Abbott:

"Master Li is a renowned artist in China. One of his paintings is decorating the Emperor's Palace and he has received the Sword of Honor."

Master lifted his hand slightly to protest my praising him, but I was too happy and proud to obey. At last I could voice out how well he had treated me, so I pleaded him to tell the Abbott exactly what I was saying and continued:

"My Master has taught me how to read and write. Without his wisdom and patience I would still be mute and totally ignorant. Not that I consider myself very wise now, but at least I am curious and eager to learn. I was unable to speak because of the horrors of the Quake, but now I have recovered from muteness. I owe my life to him."

Master shook his head and I still don't know whether he translated all I said.

The Abbott rubbed his bald head with both hands and frowned.

"You have come a long way, from Guilin! May

I ask what is your destination?"

Master replied with a broad smile:

"We are on our way to Kun Lun, the Mountain of Enlightenment."

The room was filled with silence.

Then the Abbott slowly stood up and disappeared. I looked at Master but neither of us spoke.

When he returned, an old monk with a curved back accompanied him.

"This is Lama Samdung Rinpoché. He will be able to give you some advice."

"Has he been there?" Master asked getting swiftly on his feet.

The skinny monk shook his head.

"No, but he has spoken to several pilgrims who have," the Abbott replied. "Now, if you wish, I will show you to your room. Your questions can wait till tomorrow. He must go and finish his duties. He likes to take care of animals so your yak and horses will be well cared for. The dog can stay with you."

Our room was very small but comfortable, and the monks brought us hot coals to keep us warm at night. A colorful curtain closed the doorway.

We put it aside to let the light of the yak butter lamps dance on the wall.

I felt very safe listening to the monotonous prayers of the monks.

The next morning Master invited Rinpoché for tea. We had some jasmine leaves left and the Lama's smile widened the moment he tasted the hot drink.

"This is very nice, I've never drank this kind of tea before," he said looking at the cup."

I wasn't surprised he liked it after the yak-butter tea he had probably been drinking all his life.

It was hard to guess the age of the Lama. He seemed old, really old. His face was covered with small wrinkles and his back was bent forward from a lifetime of humble prayer. His hands trembled and he walked with hesitant steps, but the twinkle in his eyes revealed the enormous life force, which maintained his skeleton body in constant move-ment. In spite of the signs time had imprinted on his shrinking body, he was ageless.

When I looked into his eyes, I suddenly under-stood he was immortal. His eyes were full of light, the kind of light death cannot put out.

"Are you immortal?" I asked, interrupting Master's explanation on the jasmine tea.

Master turned to me and I hastily apologized for my spontaneous interruption.

"Do not feel sorry for interrupting us. It is a noteworthy question and I am also interested in hearing Rinpoché's answer," Master said.

The old Lama looked at me with kindness.

"Yes. We all are immortal. Me, you, your Master, – everybody is. Even those who do not believe they are and those who think they do not deserve it. There is too much love in the universe to cast out any sentient being. It usually takes many lifetimes to become aware of whom we really are, pure, immortal, spiritual beings. When we reach perfection, we do not have to reincarnate anymore. The wheel of rebirths ends in Nirvana. We monks choose to come back to help relieve suffering on earth and to guide those who seek the Light of Kun Lun. The path of finding a better way to live is not for those who need it. It's for those who seek it."

"Can you tell us if Kun Lun is very far from here?" Master asked Rinpoché.

"You must cross the Himalayas and travel Northwest during seven moons. It is on the plateau of Tibet."

"How can we know which mountain it is the right one?"

"You will know," he said meaningfully.

⊰ ⊱

The Buddhist monks were wonderful people, and I made many friends. In their view, all prayers had the same destiny and the different ways of perceiving Tao were an exciting source of interest and enhancement to them.

One night I was drinking the remains of our jasmine tea with the Abbott, Rinpoché, some novices and Master Li.

Rinpoché brought up the subject of different religions and said:

"All religions come from one source and every person has a right to interpret the universe his own way."

"That is correct," said the Abbott. "Some people call the source God. Some call it the Great Spirit,

Universal Mind or Divine Wisdom. Others see it as a Creative Intelligence, Supreme Love, Karma or Allah. People in India see it in the millions of Gods they worship."

Rinpoché nodded his head and continued while fondling his prayer beads:

"No one can claim to possess the right view. Other people's visions enhance our understanding. Meditation and prayer has helped me grow tolerant and respectful with those who think differently."

One of the novices asked:

"How can I be tolerant when someone insists that I am wrong to believe we live many lifetimes? I can remember many things from my previous life and I have recognized my grandmother who still lives. I went to see her a year ago. She was shocked when I told her that I had misplaced a white scarf she thought she had lost. Then I showed her where it was. She had given it to me when she came to live at our house and it was a very special scarf with my name embroidered on it. Maybe those who think we live only once do not remember their past."

Master frowned and told us about a Portuguese sailor he had once met in Macao.

"He was also convinced we are only given one chance. He had been taught that those who break the laws of the Bible burn in hell for eternity, but he was sure that life here on earth was enough of an inferno. We talked about forgiveness and he said that the God of his understanding would not sentence any man to be tortured for the rest of his existence. I told him that at least the Buddhist hell, the realm of hungry ghosts, is only a temporary dwelling place. The sailor and I agreed that carrying a bad conscience, with all its side effects, is a fine punishment for wrong actions."

Then Master Li took out the Sanskrit poem from his sack and read it aloud. Rinpoché said it held the wisdom of Buddha.

Master and I meditated with the monks several times a day. I sat on a small round pillow with my legs folded on both sides. I could sit like that for hours. It was much more comfortable than trying to bend my legs into a lotus position, which – according to the monks, was not necessary anyway.

We did not need more than two or three hours

of sleep at night. I only ate vegetarian food but, to my surprise, did not lose my strong complexion. I don't know if meat makes men aggressive or not, but during that vegetarian winter I was serene and unruffled.

There were around five hundred monks living at the monastery. I had always thought that religion was a serious and solemn thing, but the monks were a joyful crowd. Their laughter echoed from the walls of stone during the day and in the evening they sang and danced in ecstasy. The dance was a cosmic dance called 'the dance of joy'. It was inspired by Milarepa, a Tibetan holy man who committed a terrible crime when he was young and then found a way to let go of his anger. Milarepa reached illumination and became a poet and an artist. Master Li admired him as one of the greatest men in history.

While the monks danced, Master explained to me that they were releasing Chi, the life force, playing with its powerful energy. He said that it was also called Prana. Then he asked me to look at the dance without focusing my eyes on anything specific. I did as he suggested and saw tiny silvery sparks around the monks. Master said that they were Chi-sparks and that I would be able to see them best in the horizon of an open landscape.

The monastery was a temporary resting place for people who had lost a loved one, who were tormented by confusion, or simply searching to expand their spiritual views. They came to find a way to deal with life's difficulties and were given clarity, no matter how deep the discomfort at the time of their arrival. When one left, another took his place.

Except for one man. With a bitter expression on his face, he was always finding fault at something.

When I asked what was wrong with him, Rinpoché said with a sigh:

"He has stayed here for years but finds no relief to his suffering. He has made misery his best friend. He likes to complain. It makes him important. He was abused as a child and he refuses to forgive his aggressor. When we do Metta, he walks out of the room. He won't let go of his resentment convinced that loving-kindness is only for the weak and stupid. He says no one can help him and as long as he believes that, he is right.

Even the Divine has difficulties to pierce through such a solid wall of pessimism. We can only pray for him."

Half a moon after Snake replaced the Dragon, Ni-hau and Ying-kha began to lose their thick winter coats. They both rubbed and scratched themselves feverishly against rocks and trees to peel off the bundles of hair hanging on their back.

My mission was to continue by my Master's side, but it was hard to say goodbye again. I had made friends at the monastery, and the winter months had been wonderfully healing. Metta had changed my feelings for MiMi's husband from hatred to compassion, and the anguish over MiMi's well-being was turned into a silent prayer.

The Abbott informed us that we would be climbing to high altitudes and that the weather would cool down considerably. He advised us to trade our horses for two yaks and let Ying-kha continue with the provisions.

We did as he suggested and set off well prepared to cross the Himalayas.

Ni-hau followed us through thick and thin. Ying-kha, perhaps aware of being close to home, advanced with enthusiasm. The two yaks we had bought were temperate and well trained for their task. When we most needed assistance, we met with a Nepalese Sherpa. His help was crucial in finding the most convenient route and we wrote it down on Zeenath's map.

Day after day and moon after moon we climbed up and down mountainsides. We burned innumerable juniper offerings to the Gods of the mountains in order to receive their blessing and permission to trespass their abode. The air was thin and we got easily tired. The rivers and valleys we crossed seemed endless. We ate whatever Ni-hau managed to find, and ran out of sweets for Ying-kha. I got the impression we were not advancing at all but, when I expressed my worries to Master, his said serenely:

"Each step takes us closer to Kun Lun. The people working in the valleys see us go forward; we appear from the East and disappear to the West. They know how far we have traveled while they watch us, but we see no progress, only the road ahead. Let's find shelter and take a break."

We found a large cave and as soon as we got in,

Ni-hau and the yaks started to behave in a strange way. They let out odd throaty growls and during the night the constant stamping of their hooves disturbed our sleep.

In the morning we noticed a tunnel inside the cave, which we had not noticed the night before. There was a faint light at the end. Master started walking towards the opening and I followed him.

Outside we saw an incredible sight. It seemed unreal, out of proportion, out of time, and out of place. Yet I recognized it.

It was Kun Lun.

The GLOWING MOUNTAIN was standing in the middle of a large frozen plateau. White clouds formed a circle around its green waist like a string of gigantic freshwater pearls. The golden peak merged into the blue sky creating a turquoise radiance. The other peaks surrounding the plateau were topped with snow and belonged to a chain of mountains, but Kun Lun stood alone, – bold, erect, and glorious.

There were white houses and green pastures at its base. Palm trees were bending their trunks over a blue lake and the cream beaches of the lake seemed to melt into the water. Multicolored flowers and fruit trees decorated the village. I could see waterfalls, rainbows and small pagodas. Tropical lagoons were almost hidden in the shade of enormous green leaves. People were rowing boats on the lake and playing with their children in the sun.

Ever since I was told there was a place for life after death, I had tried to imagine what it would be like. The sight surpassed all my fantasies.

"Master, is it real?" I whispered.

"Oh yes, but it still perplexes me to see it with my own eyes," he answered. "My faith has been put on trial several times by those self-appointed, well-meaning, all-knowing advisers who told me that I was mad to abandon my high position in pursuit of an illusive chimera. I wish they could see this!"

"Is that white village the resting place for our dead ancestors?" I asked him.

"No my dear boy. That is the Valley of Comfort, the Shangri-La of earth-bound. It was built with dreams of an easy and effortless life. The people of the village prefer material well-being to the discomfort of a spiritual path."

I looked at Kun Lun. The slope towards the peak looked impossible to climb and I began to wonder whether it was worth the trouble with such a paradise lying at its feet.

We lit a candle of gratitude for the long journey we had traveled and sat admiring the magnificent landscape. Then we started descending towards the valley.

The yaks bellowed in excitement when we rode through the snow towards the green fields ahead of us. Ying-kha straightened her ears, sniffed the air and ran as if she was carrying only a silk scarf on her back. Ni-hau gave us one short look asking for permission and dashed off.

When we got closer to the village, another wonder lay ahead; the falling snowflakes turned into drops of water and produced a thin curtain of colorful mist. The bright sun and the mist created a bright rainbow around the lush base of Kun Lun. It was a mysterious frontier between the pleasant climate of the valley and the freezing outside world.

We crossed the rainbow frontier, took off our winter clothes, and walked barefoot on the warm grass. It was a breathtaking sensation after having our tired feet imprisoned inside stiff leather boots during many, many moons. Butterflies came to fly around us when we sat down.

"Here we sit, at last!" Master said and looked at the village.

"I welcome the lazy days and pleasures of this village. We deserve a prize after the hardships we have endured on the way here. We have been on the road for over three years! But I will not stay long. I swear I will climb up that soaring peak in front of us, no matter the dangers and trials."

We let the animals enjoy the green grass and

meditated for a while before continuing.

A woman came to greet us when we got on our feet. She looked Japanese. Her face was carefully painted with white powder and her lips were like ripe cherries. She introduced herself as Ikihana. She was dressed in an elegant purple kimono with a thick silver belt. The perfume she was wearing was intoxicating and her graceful elegance seducing, but her smile brought back tender memories of MiMi.

"Welcome to the Valley of Comfort," she said in perfect Mandarin and bowed to us. "My mistress sent me as soon as she saw you in the horizon. I am from the best Palace of Pleasures in the village. We have beautiful girls from all parts of the world. Would you like to follow me?"

"Who could say no to such beauty," Master said, accepting her invitation.

I was staggered. I had always considered Master an artist and a spiritual being, – not a man who would be drawn to courtesans. But he was my Master. If he wanted to be with a woman, it was not my business to judge his actions.

Ikihana took us to a white marble palace where

there were hot thermal baths and large soft beds draped with red silk sheets. The last time I saw my Master before he disappeared for several days, he was talking with a young white girl who was carrying a silver jar, a plate of fruit, and two crystal cups.

Ikihana stayed in my room. She bathed me as if I was a baby and gave me a massage, which made me feel light as a snowflake. When she lay down beside and offered to give me more pleasure, I gently declined and fell asleep surrounded by her perfume.

In the morning she talked about her life and said:

"I came to the valley with my husband, who was a former Kung Fu Master turned opium addict. He had planned to climb Kun Lun, but ended up succumbing to his fatal addiction.

My life is nice and easy now. I receive gifts from men and they buy me all the jewels and clothes I want. I have everything I need. I am respected. I fulfill men's dreams and I lighten their burdens by just listening to their stories for a while. Then I give them what they want: sex, – a short-lived reprieve from their troubles.

I sing and dance to everyone's pleasure, including mine. What else could I possibly want? A new husband to be abandoned by again? A child to lose my figure? Struggle and go through hardships to save my soul? No, no, no. My head is well placed on my shoulders and my feet firmly on the ground. My life is here at the Palace and it's the best the world can offer. There is no life after death, so I do not care what happens when I'm dead and burned to ashes.

The stories about the wonders of Kun Lun are false. There is nothing there. I have seen many strangers like you come to this village. They try to climb the mountain and come back pale with fright. Some never return. Not one man has ever come back to say he reached the peak and found – well, whatever you're supposed to find at Kun Lun."

Her words made me feel sorry for my Master. For the first time since we left Guilin, I had serious doubts about my duty to him. Maybe it was not my mission to follow my Master to the bitter end. In addition, I wondered whether what he was doing with the girl at the mansion was morally fit for a pilgrim who was on his way to be reunited with his departed wife. On the other hand, how did I know he had accepted her favors? Maybe he had turned them down the same way I had.

⚜

I could hardly recognize my Master when he came to see me. He looked almost my age. To see him so rejuvenated confused me almost as much as the discouraging opinions of Ikihana.

"Please come with me," he said and walked out of the door.

I followed him a few feet behind, as always. He stopped at the rainbow frontier, where we could see the whole village, and turned to me.

"Yu, I want you to take a good look around, for you can stay here if you wish. You have worked hard for many years and helped me come this far. People here work only if they want to, for there is enough food and necessities for everybody. The valley has a wonderful climate and it is surrounded by beauty. It has all you need to lead a pleasant and comfortable existence. Here you might find happiness. Maybe you can marry and have children. You owe me nothing and I cannot ask you to continue with me. If you choose to stay, Tao will continue to guide you and my prayers will always be with you."

I watched the inhabitants of the valley in their everyday routine. They where living in an orderly community with no apparent problems. They ate, and slept, and raised their children. They rowed little boats on the river, picked fruit from the trees and visited friends.

It seemed a tempting way to live.

Then it dawned on me that something was wrong; time stood still in the Valley of Comfort. Life was stagnant. There was nothing to strive for. There were no books in the village; nobody read anything. Music was absent and birds knew no songs. People of the valley did not want to discover truths, reveal mysteries or expand their minds. They had no other goal in life but to live a comfortable existence – while Kun Lun stood right in front of their eyes. They denied their spirit the right for fulfillment. They had abandoned their mission.

I looked into my Master's calm eyes and said:

"What I see here is very tempting indeed. Iki-hana said at the Palace of Pleasures that Kun Lun is a myth and that she had never seen any man come back from the peak. Her words made me doubt for a while. But the things you have taught me since I was a child have sunk deep in my heart. Life with you has awakened my thirst for wisdom and peace of mind. It's too late to stay. Besides, my mission is to serve you and I'd rather fight a hundred monsters than abandon my duty."

Master bowed to me and said smiling:

"Masters become pupils and pupils turn to masters. I need to say something before we set off; if something happens to me on the way to Kun Lun keep the gold we have. I have no need for it where I will go. Now, is there anything you would like me to do in case I must return without you?"

I had to think. My life was simple. I was just a servant. I had no possessions and no business to worry about. There was nothing I would leave behind if I died – except my earthly remains. I discovered though that I did have a wish.

"Yes," I replied. "Continue your journey and

leave my body to nourish vultures and other animals."

"I will not fail your request," he said.

Before we left we freed Ying-kha, who was seemingly happy in the green fields of the valley. If she missed the cold temperatures, she could cross the rainbow curtain and wallow in the snow whenever she wanted. Master thought that Ni-hau should also stay in the safety of the village. I felt a cramp in my stomach when he said that. I had forgotten the monsters of Kun Lun. I agreed she was better off in the village in case something happened to us.

We thanked and blessed Ni-hau, Ying-kha and the other two yaks. I had not been aware of how good a friend Ni-hau had become until it was time to say farewell. With her tail hanging sadly down, she walked to the Palace of Pleasures, and lay down with her head between the paws. Her brightness in her amber eyes grew dim as she watched us depart.

ThERE WAS only a narrow path leading upwards. Step by step, the green pastures sank further and further behind us, but we never lost them from sight.

"The Valley of Comfort is there to tempt us in case we get discouraged. We can always return if we decide to give up." Master Li said looking back.

We had climbed for seven days when we came to a rusty iron gate and I heard a frightening roar. The sun was setting, so we camped on the platform in front of the gate. I was prepared for some terrible appearance, but nothing happened.

I fell asleep and had a dream:

A fire-spitting monster with seven heads and gleaming eyes was guarding the Gate of Fear. I heard deep growling voices coming from each head:

"I am the guardian of this gate. What do you want?"

I felt a lump in my throat.

"I want to pass through the gate."

"Would you still want to pass if I told you that I will tear you apart with my seven jaws and eat you alive?"

Keep it simple and tell the truth, I remembered Master's words. But what was my truth? Was I willing to risk my life to help my Master?

"You do your duty, I will do mine," I answered. "My feet tremble and the horrors of being eaten alive scare me. But I shall not allow my fear to divert me from what is important to me. My mission is to help my Master find his wife and reach enlightenment. I seek to pass through the gate, eat me if you must."

The monster's eyes turned inside out and, accompanied with a terrible roar, it turned into a rock.

The following morning Master told me he had had the same dream.

"What was your answer?" I asked him.

"That I was willing to die rather than give up my quest."

"And the monster turned into a rock?"

"Yes, roaring with pain."

We both looked around and saw no iron gate. Yesterday it was there and now it was gone. There was a huge rock in its place with a path leading around it.

We prayed and lit a candle of gratitude.

Master explained that candles help prayers rise up to heaven, where they are united with all other prayers. There they wait and accumulate force. When they have enough power, they fall upon earth and produce miracles. One simple prayer of thanksgiving can be the one needed to release their might.

We climbed for six days and came to an old iron gate. There were shrieking sounds coming from above us. We camped in front of the gate and I fell asleep shivering with fear.

I dreamt of six black vultures with enormous bloody beaks circling over my head. The sky turned purple as they screamed:

"We are the guardians of the Gate of Doubt. There is nothing at the peak of Kun Lun. Go back to the Valley of Comfort or we will tear you apart and eat you alive."

I stopped to think.

I remembered Zeenath, the jolly merchant, and

his story about a naked saint. I heard the gloomy words of Ikihana. I thought about the wisdom of Master Li and the power of Tao.

"You may be right," I said. "There may be nothing worthwhile at the end of this road. However, I have chosen to walk this path — even if it leads nowhere. I believe there is a better way to live and a chance I may find it along the way. My Master says that it's better to seek and find nothing than not to seek at all. Do as you must."

I was surprised at my own conviction. The words I spoke affirmed my faith in the wonders of Kun Lun.

The vultures let out terrible shrieks, fell to the ground and turned into six stones.

The following morning Master told me he had had the same dream.

"What did you say to them?" I asked him.

"That I believe in miracles and that I'd rather return empty handed than turn back."

The gate we had seen the night before had disappeared and there were six small stones in front of us. We prayed and left a candle of gratitude on each stone.

It took us five days to reach the next gate.

There was a frightening silence when I went to sleep. I dreamt of five dreadful ghosts whirling around me. One of them touched me with its dead-cold hand and said:

"We are the guardians of the Gate of Guilt. We know who you are. We know the secrets of your past. You have committed terrible offenses. We have come to drag you into the shadows with us, where you shall be tortured for five eons."

I understood only too well what they were talking about. I had done bad things during my life, and the ghosts had come to punish me.

As a young boy, I had stolen money from an old woman at the market, who had asked me to guard her fruit stand while she went to do chores. Instead of protecting her property, I had robbed her of two silver coins. The incident had been weighing on my conscious for years.

Then I had once visited a courtesan. When she had asked me more than I could afford for her favors, I had made insulting gestures towards her and spat on her face.

On several occasions I had lied to Master Li saying I was not feeling well, when I was too lazy to do what he asked.

I had once taken a bottle of rose liquor from Master's wine cellar and gotten drunk with his nephew Jei-ming. We had wrestled in the living room and broken a valuable vase Master Li had bought in Nanking. I was so afraid of my Master's anger that I told him it had been stolen.

The worst offense was recent and it tormented me deeply: I had prayed for the death of MiMi's husband.

I bowed my head in shame and whispered:

"I am guilty of the offenses you refer to. I am a bad person. Take me with you. I have no right to walk the road to Kun Lun."

As I looked up, the ghosts turned into luminous beings and I heard a gentle voice:

"You have admitted your faults and confessed the misdeeds you have committed. You are filled with shame. You are not evil. Evil regrets nothing. Let your guilt stay here and continue forward."

The gate flung open and I woke up.

Master Li had had the same dream but we both kept silent about our answers to the ghosts. I felt relief after admitting things I had kept secret for years, but could not say them out loud to my Master.

We lit candles of gratitude and continued in silence.

彐 ⺕

Four days later we found another closed gate and I smelled something burning. We looked for a fire but saw nothing. I fell asleep and had a dream:

There were four burning arrows pointing at me. I knew they had something to do with the wrong-doing I had confessed to the ghosts. As I looked at the arrows, images of the people I had hurt came to my mind – the old woman at the market, the courtesan and Master Li.

I also saw my own face next to them.

I heard a voice:

"We are the guardians of the Gate of Amends. These arrows are you're negative Karma. They are waiting to be shot at you. You cannot pass unless you apologize and make amends for the harm you have done.

"But how can I do that?" I cried in despair. "The old woman is far away, there's no way I can pay back the money I stole! The courtesan moved to Beijing and I'll never find her to ask for her forgiveness! And... oh help me Tao, I do not know what my Master will do to me if he finds out what I have done!"

"Then live with guilt and fear."

I woke up covered with sweat. Master was sitting next to me and the gate remained closed.

"Did you also dream of arrows with burning heads?" He asked me.

"Yes. I feel terrible, but I do not want to carry guilt. I want you to know that I have lied to you and broken your vase."

I told him the details of my actions and asked him to pardon me. He did something he had never done.

He embraced me.

Then he said:

"I could have saved a man's life during the Quake. Instead of rescuing him I just sat and watched him die. The incident has been tormenting me ever since. Once I sought help from a wise old medicine man. He explained that a tragedy can produce such a profound mental apathy that we let go. Our mind stands still and gives no orders for the body to move. He said I should not blame myself for the death of that man, but I do.

The most difficult apologies are made face to face. I have wronged you by thinking that I am better and wiser than you. Sometimes I have treated you harshly. I am very sorry."

I had nothing to forgive him. He was my Master and it was his duty to be severe. He took some candles out from his sack and said:

"No matter how far away the people we have harmed are right now, there is no distance between us – even if they are dead. Metta will help us reach them and express our regrets. It will also help us to forgive ourselves.

We lit a candle for each person we needed to make amends to and prayed aloud for their well-being, happiness, and freedom from suffering. It was a long, intense, and sincere prayer, during which I felt deep remorse.

When I opened my eyes I felt wonderful. The gate was open.

Master was still on his knees and said:

"I feel as if the whole universe has forgiven me for not

being perfect. I no longer feel guilt and shame."

"I also feel liberated from all my burdens." I said and thanked him for teaching me the Metta prayer.

We left five candles of gratitude next to each arrow.

⊰ ⊱

Our steps were light and our spirits renewed. We continued our climb during three days until there was a silver gate in front of us. No roars, no shrieks – nothing to indicate danger. We camped outside and I fell asleep.

During the night I heard a friendly voice:

"This the Gate of Prayer. It will be open when you wake up, for you know how to pray and practice daily. To be thankful for blessings received – and those yet to come – is to practice the awareness of Tao. But, since you have many times wondered why your prayers are not answered, we want to remind you that the universe unfolds, as it should. When you ask for yourself, you may be praying for things that are not beneficial for you. When you pray for someone else – no matter how good your intentions – you may not be aware of what is best for him. Tao knows. So pray and let go."

We woke up and the gate was open. There was no need to ask each other about the voice, we knew we had both heard it.

We lit three candles of gratitude and sat meditating for a while.

"We often do not see how far we have come," said Master when we got on our feet. "We tend to focus on all those things we have not yet learned, instead of seeing the accomplished and appreciating the efforts and courage we have put in. However, the work is done."

⊰ ⊱

Two days passed and we arrived at another silver gate. There were three clouds over the gate; one was a bright white cloud and the other two were black. I fell asleep to sounds of thunder.

In my dream I saw images of my past life flow in front of me. I was reminded of all those things that brought me pain; the friends I had left behind, the opportunities I had lost; the mistakes I had made; and the happy times I had spent with MiMi. In the next scene, I entered a suffocating room. The walls were painted with the images of my worst fears; the things that had not yet happened but could, tangled around me like a thick, sticky spider's web.

I heard a voice:

"Do you wish to pass this gate?"

"Yes," I replied.

"Then you must let go of everything that belongs to your past or your future. In return, I shall give you the Awareness of the Present Moment. It is a gift. That's why it is called the Present. When you dwell in yesterday, or when your happiness depends on what will happen tomorrow, you are blind to the magic of today. With full Awareness of the Present Moment you let go of everything and live in the here and now."

I lowered my head and said:

"If I give you my past and my future, what shall I do empty handed? Many good things have happened to me and I like to remember them. Where will I end up if I have no dreams to fulfill? I want to help my Master reach the peak."

"To live wholeheartedly is to give up worrying about things gone by and those yet to be. I shall not take away your memories and you may keep your dreams. I am not asking you to let go of your efforts, only the results they may have."

"But I'll be very unhappy if I fail to reach the peak!"

"Bitterness, resentments and fear are always chained to yesterday's disappointments and expectations of tomorrow. To live in the Present is to give up those burdens. It is to accept life as it is at this very moment."

As I listened to the voice I understood, that every time I wanted to go back to some happiness I had felt, or regretted things that had happened, I was frustrated. Life was moving forward and it was impossible to go back. The good times and the bad times I had were gone forever. And each time I tried to imagine what was waiting for me around the corner, I got distressed. The future was an unwritten page in the Book of Life. It was written only one page at a time. I concluded that it was more important to enjoy life's journey than to arrive at a goal.

I opened my palms in a gesture of giving and said:

"Take all I have, take all that I've been holding on to with tight fists. I long to travel light with no regrets and no false hopes. Take all that is preventing me from living in the here and now."

Suddenly I was aware of Master being by my side. He was on his knees, clinging to TaiTai's portrait, crying out loud:

"But how can I let go of my love? I want to be united with her. She is the only reason why I am here! I cannot give you what you ask of me. I cannot give away the happiness we have shared, thought it has given me much sorrow after I lost her. I can not let go of the bliss I will find when we meet again!"

There was a silence at the Gate of the Present.

When I woke up in the morning, my Master was lying on his back and the light of his eyes was gone. His face hair had turned completely white and he was holding his wife's portrait against his chest with clasped hands.

The sky was clear and the gate open.

I jerked up, ran to him, grabbed him by his robe, and lifted him up. Shaking his lifeless body in the air I cried out:

"Master, you must let go! You cannot die, we are too close to the peak!"

My words echoed around the rocks: "Peak now, now, no…"

I fell to the ground with him and whispered:

"With all your wisdom… I never thought you would die and fail to see the Light of Kun Lun!"

The sun went down and I sat by his body. I didn't know what to do. There was no one to give me instructions on how to deal with the emptiness I was experiencing.

My Master was gone.

When it got dark, my sorrow turned to anger.

What a waste of wisdom with such a cruel end! What awful injustice! Master only wanted to be united with his wife. He was a good man. He deserved it. And I had the right to my mission. This world is an ugly, atrocious place. Dreams are shattered and loved ones lost; possessions robbed, promises broken; friends come and go. Loneliness and pain all life through! No wisdom to deal with heartaches and no defense against violence. No reward for a man who tries to do his best. No use to strive to be happy. A moment of joy leaves you nothing but a lifetime of longing. All is lost, sooner or later. What a useless path. Ikihana was right; the road to Kun Lun leads nowhere. How stupid and meaningless is the Tao!

"Eat me alive, you monsters of Kun Lun!" I cried out loud. "I wish I had never been born!"

I fell asleep exhausted and had a dream:

I was a little drop of water among many others and together we formed the River of Life. The River had a direction and all other drops were flowing peacefully to the unknown. But I was swimming against the current. I was trying to control the flow and change the course of the River. I struggled and

fought, convinced that I was an especially powerful water drop. When I had no energy left to fight,
I surrendered defeated, humiliated, and filled with
bitter disappointment. I blamed myself for the
failure and came to the conclusion that, since I
had not succeeded in my task to turn the mighty
waters, I was somehow flawed. But as soon as I let
go, I felt an overwhelming sensation of relief. I was
one with the River. No matter the winding ways,
it would take me home. I saw my fellow water
drops glow in the sun and understood that I was
like them. I was born to radiate the colors of the
rainbow. I jumped high up in the air, filled with
the glory and wonder of being a water drop. And
at that moment, before merging into the infinite
sea, I saw the beauty of the world.

I woke up renewed.

I was on the road to Kun Lun; I was floating in
the River of Life. To be there was no longer my
duty. It was a privilege.

Master's body was lying by my side, pale and
stiff.

I was his servant and could still do something for
him that he could no longer do himself: I would

carry him with me.

He wasn't very heavy, but the slope was steep. The gold around my waist and his weight on my shoulders made climbing difficult. Many times I fell to the ground and his body rolled down the slope. But, each time I got up and lifted him back on my shoulders, I felt as if it were the first time we had fallen.

I was only aware of each step that I took.

⚜

When the day ended and stars appeared in the sky, I came to a golden gate. I lay my Master on the ground and fell asleep.

I dreamt of a white Goddess, who was holding in her hand a Ray of Light. She was pointing at the gate and said:

"I am the guardian of the Gate of Power. Behind this gate there is enough Hope, Trust and Faith to last a lifetime. If you were to receive the Power of Tao, what would you with it?"

I didn't have to think twice.

"I lost all I had in the Quake. My Master gave

me a new life and awakened my spirit and I am deeply grateful for what he gave me. I would grant him what he sought: The Light of Kun Lun."

"You ask nothing for yourself. Why?"

"Because Tao gives me all I need."

After a long silence she spoke again:

"I shall give you a new mission: Take this Ray of Light and give it to any man, woman or child who comes to you and asks for it. It's not yours for the keeping. Pass it on."

"But how will people know I have it? What if nobody comes to me?" I asked puzzled.

"Many are in need of it. But those who do not want it will not come to you, and you must not interfere with the way they are being prepared to ask for it. The ones who are ready will find you and approach you. They know what you have. And they will have the courage to ask and the willingness to receive."

I remembered the people who left the Monastery of the Golden Buddha renewed, whereas one poor man was not willing to find peace.

There was one more thing I wanted to know:

"Why me?"

"Because you are a servant," the goddess replied. I agreed to follow her instructions and she gave me the Ray of Light.

I woke up in the morning and the gate was open. My hand was radiating with bright light.

After lighting a candle of gratitude I lifted Master on my shoulders and continued our journey.

⊰ ⊱

I was out of breath and lay Master Li on the ground. We had reached a point where the clouds formed such a thick fog that I could not see anything.

Suddenly I heard a soft voice:

"Take my hand."

I saw nothing in the fog, but I was aware of a strangely familiar presence. Then a Luminous Being appeared by my side. She had wings of a swan and her feet didn't touch the ground.

"Who are you?" I asked.

"I am the spirit of your Master's garden."

Then she put her palms together, crossed the middle fingers and moved them like wings of a bird.

The secret sign! Master needs help and his wife comes to him.

I took her hand. It was a warm, gentle hand, yet it filled me with incredible strength. We climbed hand in hand and I put one foot in front of the other, trusting she knew the way.

When sunbeams broke through the thick fog, I noticed the Luminous Being was not with me anymore and my hand was empty. I wondered if I had imagined her presence or if she had really come to my rescue.

I looked around.

The golden peak of Kun Lun was still far away and the clouds around the mountain formed a soft platform at my feet. Further down lay the Valley of Comfort. In spite of the lush tropical greenery, it seemed to have lost its allure. It looked grim.

The peak was shining against the clear blue sky. I realized I still had a long climb ahead.

It will take days to get up! I thought. Maybe I'll never get there!

Then I remembered a story Master had once told me:

'A lion was pursuing a man and drove him to the

edge of a cliff. There was no way to escape except by jumping to a certain death. The man accepted his fate and knelt down in surrender. Suddenly he noticed there were roots at his feet. The roots lead downward and served as a ladder. He began to descend. However, when he looked down, there was a bear waiting for him on the ground. He was caught between a roaring lion up on the cliff and a growling bear down on the ground, but he looked neither way. He studied the spot he was at and found strawberries growing right beside him. Delighted, he started to eat them, one by one. They were ripe and sweet. When there were no more strawberries left he looked up. The lion had given up and left. The bear was gone too. He descended safely and went home.'

I looked down at the Valley of Comfort and the far away peak of Kun Lun. I was at a perfect spot. I was aware of the peaceful moment. I was safe.

I sat down and closed my eyes. There was a faint, soothing humming in the air and I fell into a deep state of meditation.

When I opened my eyes I was standing at the peak of Kun Lun. My Master was lying at my feet and the Luminous Being was by his side.

She covered him with a shining veil and I watched in wonder how Master slowly left his dead body. A warm breeze blew over the peak when their spirits intertwined and became one.

I was awestruck. A beautiful light surrounded me and I reached out to it. The moment I touched it with my fingertips, all the pain on earth – the suffering of each plant and animal, the sorrows of every human being – was reflected in my soul. I saw the past and the future. I was filled with understanding and compassion. Loving Tao embraced me and I saw the Perfect Unity of All Things. There was only Endless Love. Nothing else existed.

And Love was the Source from which Eternity was flowing.

It was the Year of the Snake and the ordinary silence in the Valley of Comfort was broken by sharp barks. The dog sitting on the stairs of the Palace of Pleasures dashed off wagging its tail.

A man was descending Kun Lun.

WhƏN I crossed the rainbow barrier, Ni-hau jumped at me and almost knocked me down. People hurried from all corners of the village to meet me, and a large crowd soon surrounded me. They looked at me with suspicion and curiosity.

"Who are you?" Someone asked.

"My name is Yu. I am a servant." I replied.

"He's carrying Li Wang's sack! Where's your Master?" I heard questions in the multitude.

I pointed towards Kun Lun.

"Show us what you have in the sack," said the man who had spoken first.

I took the flute, the Sanskrit proverb, and the gold from Master's sack and placed it on the ground.

The crowd shouted:

"Look at all that gold! He has killed and robbed his Master! We cannot let him get away with it!"

Ni-hau started to growl. The crowd formed a tight circle around us. A woman screamed:

"We must protect our children! He must be put in the cave!"

Ni-hau's yellow eyes were burning and she growled, showing her teeth.

The crowd took a few steps back. By then, the leaders of the Valley had arrived at the scene. They ordered me to be thrown into the cave of penitence and chained to the wall so I would not escape. Ni-hau was captured with fishing net and taken away.

After a short meeting, the Valley Council announced that I was guilty of murder and condemned to death. The sentence was to be carried out by sword at dawn.

I felt no fear, for I knew they could do as they pleased with my body, but no one could harm my soul.

I was immortal.

While I slept in peace and warmth on the cold floor of the cave, something happened outside.

The menacing purple of the sunset had already been a bad omen, and the night brought with it an unexpected disaster upon the Valley of Comfort. Torrential storms and freezing winds blew through the village. Palm trees were covered with thick frost, green pastures buried under heaps of snow, and the lake turned into an icy mirror of the calamity.

The villagers rushed to see me before sunrise.

"Make it go away!" they yelled. "Make it go away, or we shall all perish in this arctic cold! We know only about living a comfortable life. We have no tools with which to resolve such problems!"

From the back of the crowd, a man emerged. "We need what this man has," the man said and addressed the Council. "We have brought disaster upon ourselves with our ignorance."

I smiled at him and asked him to bring me my Master's sack. He brought it and gave it to me. The man bowed to me and said:

"I am Manu, the Spanish gardener of the valley."

"Ah, Spaniard. Good. I met your countrymen in a caravan," I said and took out the Sanskrit poem.

I asked Manu to read it.

"This is worth a hundred books of worldly wisdom!" he exclaimed after he finished.

Then he read it out loud:

"Look to this day…"

He turned to the crowd and said:

"We have not lived well. The actions we took yesterday have not brought bliss, splendor and glory. On the contrary! After we condemned this man, our Valley was buried under ice and our gardens are dying. If we carry out the sentence now we shall all perish." Holding the poem aloft he spoke, "Here it says we can take a different path today. Our tomorrow depends on what we do at this moment."

The poem was translated to those who could not understand and Manu gave it back to me.

I tried to get on my feet, but the chains were so short that I fell down. I noticed Manu bend his head down in shame as I read on my knees:

"Look well, therefore, to this day."

A light appeared above my head, and the crowd receded a few steps back.

"This man is incapable of murdering anyone," Manu said. "We must let him go. Besides, who are we to deny anyone the right to live?"

The Council was called for an urgent session.

They came back announcing that the only way to save the valley was to set me free. The chains were removed and Master Li Wang's gold and possessions returned to me. Ni-hau was waiting for me when I walked out of the cave. Nevertheless,

I was told that I disturbed the peace of the village and the Council asked me to leave as soon as possible. There was no room for the unknown in the Valley of Comfort.

However, having been impressed by the occurrences, the Council decided that the death penalty was no longer to be used as punishment.

The frozen valley recovered its tropical climate.

⚜

When I was preparing to leave, Manu came to see me. He bowed with respect and said:

"I came to this valley with the intention of conquering Kun Lun. I've been tending the gardens for six long months, gathering courage to start climbing. Every night I say: tomorrow I'll start climbing. In the morning I wake up and again say: I'll do it tomorrow.

After seeing you on your knees at the cave I realized that I have no need to go to Kun Lun. You are illuminated. You have what I want. If I stay close to you, I may find the light I'm seeking. Please be my teacher and let me accompany you. I will serve and protect you on your journey, wherever it leads. I'm willing to leave the easy life in this valley and seek peace for my soul. Today, not 'mañana'."

His words touched me deeply and I bowed back to him. Then I thanked him for defending me at the cave of penitence and said:

"What was revealed to me at the top of Kun Lun can neither be taught nor described, for it's the result of walking one's own path. But the light is yours for the asking."

I placed the Ray of Light in his hand and noticed that I still had mine left. It had split into two lights, which seemed even brighter than the original one.

"Give it away to any man, woman or child who comes to you and asks for it. It's not yours for the keeping. Pass it on."

He looked at the Light mesmerized and I continued:

"It would be a pleasure to have you share my journey, but I am not a Master of anything. I am a simple servant, so please call me Yu. You can serve me best by being my friend. A fellow traveler enriches life and helps change old beliefs to new ones. Being alone is sometimes good. Being lonely is not."

My Spanish wasn't very fluent and I was happy Manu understood the language of the heart. Then I laughed at what he had said earlier and referred to his self-criticism:

"Manu my friend, we are not leaving today. Our departure is 'mañana'."

I decided we would ride the same yaks Master Li and I had arrived with, and load Ying-kha with provisions. I would leave her in Katmandu at the Monastery of the Golden Buddha. Ni-hau jumped around nipping my feet when I mounted my yak.

The valley people were relieved to see us leave. They did not want to change their comfortable lives, even if it was for the better.

They had found happiness in the way they lived.

WheN We started climbing over the Himalayas and the Valley of Comfort disappeared from sight I said to Manu:

"I am returning to Guilin. Master Li and I left his house three years ago, but we stopped for long periods of time on the way here. It is possible we will make the journey in two years. What is your religion?"

"I'm a Catholic, but I like the idea of being granted many lifetimes. It seems logical and fair. It's the only way I can explain the seemingly unfair suffering in this world. I believe I am responsible for where I am today."

"Do you know what Tao is?" I asked him.

"No."

"Tao is the beginning and the end. It is the river and the sea."

"I have no idea what you are talking about." Manu said downcast.

"Oh, now I remember, the golden necklaces with saints! Let's see... I will keep it simple and use the word 'God' to replace what I would call the Power of Tao. It will help you understand what I mean. Tell me about yourself."

We rode side by side and Manu began his story:

"You know by now that my name is Manu. It's actually Pedro Manuel Uceta de Polavieja, but everybody calls me Manu. I'm twenty-one years old and I come from Toledo, where my parents own a tavern. I'm here because of a painting I once found at the market. It represents a beautiful monastery in a valley surrounded by snowy peaks. I had always fantasized about going there one day.

Well… I was working at the tavern when a foreigner came to eat. He sat there the whole evening. When the clients had left and I started to clean the tables, he showed no signs of wanting to leave. He had traveled alone for a long time and just needed someone to talk to so I let him stay. He had come to Toledo to sell fine silk carpets. He told me some amazing stories, and I was spellbound by one of them. He said he had met a holy man who had climbed some mysterious Himalayan mountain and found a treasure. It wasn't money or anything like that, the foreigner said, – the man had found his soul.

The merchant came to the tavern every day and, although he was much older than I was, we became friends.

One day I asked him what was his next destination and he said:

'Oh, back home to count my children! With three wives I never know how many new babies I have until I arrive. I haven't seen my family for months. I miss the food and the good service too! When I'm home, the children climb all over me like monkeys. That's how I spend a month or two, eating, making love and playing with my children. Totally happy! Then I load my wagon with carpets and leave again.'

I asked him where was 'home' and he said he lived in Kashmir, at the foot of the Himalayas. I showed him the painting I had hung on the wall of the tavern and asked if
he had seen anything like it. He said that there were many
places like that at the foot of the Himalayas.

The Himalayas, Yu! What a strange coincidence. I had wanted to see a place like the one in the painting and the merchant lived close by. When he left Toledo, I left with him. He helped me earn enough silver to pay for the journey. That's how I got to the Valley of Comfort."

"Was the merchant's name Zeenath?" I asked.

He looked stunned.

"How would you know that?"

"Master Li and I met him on our way here. He told us about the holy man too. He sold us a map and his yak... Ying-kha. Master Li drew on the map the route we took here; we will go back the same way. Zeenath guided us both to Kun Lun, but it was not by accident. There are no coincidences. God guides us through the people we meet. Everything is connected and has meaning. In the apparent chaos, there is perfect order."

⠀⠀⠀⠀⠀⠀⠀⠀⠀⠀⠀⠀⠀≒⠀≒

To protect our eyes, we avoided traveling through snow while the skies were clear and the sun shone brightly. The Sherpa appeared again to help us, and we crossed the Himalayas performing the same rituals as on our way to Kun Lun.

Finally we saw from afar the Monastery of the Golden Buddha.

Manu cried out with excitement:

"This looks like the painting! The one I told you about!"

I smiled and continued descending.

The way my monk friends welcomed me was very embarrassing. They threw themselves flat on the ground a dozen times. Even the Abbott greeted me that way and ordered a special ceremony for the night of our arrival.

In the evening all the monks gathered in the large prayer hall. The Abbott asked me to share my journey and the light I had received.

It was difficult to talk due to my limited vocabulary. I had barely started to tell my story, when the Ray of Light in my hand suddenly began to cast familiar images on the altar in front of us. Without the need to speak, my journey was exposed to the monks, exactly as it happened. But the images stopped at the moment I touched the Light of Kun Lun.

I tried to explain that I had been face to face with Tao and that for a timeless moment I was shown all past things and those yet to come. I said that I had shared the immense suffering of the world, as if it was my own, and that it had increased my love and compassion.

Then I spoke in my own language and the words seemed to flow:

"I discovered that everything in our world, and beyond, belongs to the perfect Unity of All Things. I felt immense peace and a sense of belonging, and lost concept of myself as a separate entity. I became free."

The Abbott brought a box and took out a Yellow Hat.

Accompanied by the sounds of blaring trumpets and low humming of the monks, he placed it on my head. Everybody present threw themselves on the ground again in worship, Manu included.

I looked at them with love in my heart and said:

"The universe unfolds as it should, no matter what we do, but our actions may change the course of someone's life. I was granted this Ray of Light only to give it away when asked. When I accepted the mission, it brought new meaning to my life. But I am still a simple servant. I thank you for your honors. Now please let me sit among you as a fellow traveler on his way home."

The monks got up and we all started to dance.

I let my body move uncontrolled. It started spinning around. It spun and spun and spun, and I felt a powerful energy flow. I remembered what Master Li had explained about Chi and how to let it flow. I got the impression that Master was with me, guiding me, sharing my dance.

The man who had made anger his best friend was still at the monastery. Knowing I could solve his problem, I asked to meet him.

He sat with me for an entire evening complaining and wallowing in self-pity. He moaned about the injustice of the world, because nothing he had prayed for himself had happened. I asked him if he had ever thought of asking for guidance to end his misery, but he replied saying that since no one had fulfilled his desires, there was nothing to ask guidance from. As much as I would have liked to, I was not allowed to give him the Ray of Light.

He had to go on suffering until the day he would have no strength left to hold on to it.

　　🙐 🙕

I started to teach Manu meditation but, in spite of

his willingness to learn, he found it very difficult to relax and let go. He said he had always been restless and that it may have been because of his Spanish blood. He said his thoughts always ran wild and his body felt uneasy. He told me he had the sensation of being in some kind of an inner hurry all the time.

"Where am I so anxious to go?" he asked me.

"I don't know. Would you like to be somewhere else?" I asked in return.

"No."

"Are you happy with your life?"

"I think so."

"Is there something you would like to change, something you desire?"

"Oh yes, many things! I'd like to be wise and skilled. It would be nice to be able to play some musical instrument. I wish I had more peace and kindness in my heart. And if I could only sit still, I would learn meditation much quicker!"

I smiled and said:

"Then you are not happy with the way things are right now. Your desires are fine goals to strive for and there is nothing wrong in moving forward to better things. However, desire is the root of all suffering. When we want what we don't have, our mind is troubled. I shall give you a task; go and write a list of everything that is well in your life. Put down on paper all the valuable things you have in your life today; things you are grateful for."

Manu went and wrote down all he could think of.

When he read it aloud, I nodded in approval and said:

"I suggest you read it, many times a day, until it becomes a constant prayer. You can add more things to it if you discover any new reasons for gratitude. Now lets see what was on your wish list: wisdom, peace, kindness, skills, sitting still... and play some musical instrument. When you want something you must define it and make sure it will cause no pain to others. Exactly what skills do you want to have?"

Manu was silent for a moment and said:

"Well, one would be enough for the moment. It's linked to another wish; I would like to play a musical instrument."

"Good. It is impossible to obtain everything you

want in one day. It takes many lessons to learn. Take this and go find someone who can teach you."

I handed him Master Li's flute and added:

"It cost my Master three years of learning and a lifetime of practice to play it. You can start today – or 'mañana'."

Manu found an old woman who was willing to teach him and started taking lessons every day. I suggested he try Metta for the rest of his wish list and assured him that he would learn how to sit still if he practiced it.

I was longing to hear the beautiful sounds of a flute, but during the first six moons I put wax in my ears as soon as he started to play.

BEFORE saying goodbye to my monk friends, I thanked the yaks for taking me across the Himalayas twice. Then I went for a long walk with Ying-kha. I told her she would be happier with the monks in her natural habitat than in the heat of Guilin. I am convinced she understood me.

The Abbott exchanged the yaks for three horses and the night before we left the monastery we danced till midnight.

At the moment of departure the monks threw themselves at my feet again. I thanked them for teaching me a valuable lesson by ignoring my wish to be treated as an equal: I have no power to make others act according to my desires.

We rode through valleys and villages for several moons. The Year of the Horse brought a good monsoon. When it rained heavily, Ni-hau hunted for food while we stayed inside the tent.

One day Manu said:

"You are very quiet lately. Have I offended you in some way?"

I was surprised at his question, until I remembered how I had felt when Master Li was troubled. In my self-centeredness I had thought it was because I had done something wrong. Manu's words helped me understand that it had not been about me; Master's mind had not been at peace. Neither was mine at that moment.

"You have done nothing wrong dear friend. I feel unease because we are getting close to the village were I met a woman who still holds my heart. The monks called me an enlightened human being, but at this moment I am only human. I do not know what to do."

"Well, if you love her, why don't you take her to Guilin with us?"

"She is property of another man."

"Married you mean?"

"Yes, to a man who does not treat her well."

"Does she love you?"

"When does a man know what a woman thinks?" I asked in return.

"You always ask me to listen to my heart. What does your heart say about her?"

I listened to my inner voice and replied:

"You have solved my problem. I shall go and see her."

We were standing on a hillside, gazing down at

the valley where MiMi lived. I asked Manu to take the horse with provisions and ride alone to the other side of the valley. I thought he should wait for me there, for I had no idea what the husband would do.

Ni-hau descended with me and her company reassured me. I was not afraid for my own sake; it was MiMi's safety I worried about.

Before reaching the village, I stopped to pray and meditate until my mind calmed down. Then I rode straight to MiMi's house.

She was not there and I was told to go to her parents' house.

The moment I saw her, love and passion returned to my veins as if I had never been away. She was hanging clothes in the front yard. Her hair was short and she was wearing a veil. As soon as she recognized me, she started banging her tiny fists against her chest in a gesture of agony. I walked slowly to her but found no words to say. She looked at me with sad eyes and lifted the veil, which was covering her face.

Upon seeing her scars I fell on my knees. She knelt beside me and embraced me.

With tears rolling down her blemished cheeks she said:

"After you left, someone told my husband about your visits. Blinded by fury, he poured coconut oil over me and set it aflame. Then he threw me out of his house. My parents took me back even though I had brought shame to their house, but I wished I had never lived; an abandoned woman's fate is worse than death. Seeing you today has brought me back to life."

"MiMi," I said with a thin voice and realized she was shocked at hearing me speak. "Oh, I have so many things to tell you!"

She nodded eagerly.

I told her I needed to speak to her parents. She took me by the hand and led me inside the house. They were both in.

I bowed to them with respect and said:

"I would like to take your daughter with me."

I knew that I had to offer them something in return; a woman had to be bought from the person who owned her.

MiMi was no longer property of her husband and now her parents had legal rights to decide her fate.

I took half of the gold from my waist bag and placed it on the table. They were speechless. There was more gold in front of them than the richest man of the village would make in years.

MiMi's father turned to her and asked:

"Do you have anything to say?"

She shook her head, yet her smile revealed she was happy.

"Then I shall fetch the Eldest of the Village," her father concluded.

We were wed in a simple ceremony after the dinner.

MiMi's father was Chinese and her mother was from Burma. They were humble folk and could not read or write. When I paid the Eldest for his services, I asked him to assist MiMi's parents to read the letters MiMi would be sending them.

Guilin was our destination, but I did not know where we would settle down. I believed Tao would guide us to the place where I could best serve the Ray of Light.

⚔ ⚔

Manu was waiting for us on the other side of the valley. He hurried to greet us and said:

"The sun went down and I was worried about you. I thought it would not be wise to make a fire, so I sat and waited in the darkness. Suddenly I heard galloping noises approaching and I felt someone jump on me. I tried to crawl away but felt a stinking, warm tongue lick my face." He burst out laughing. "It was Ni-hau."

"This is MiMi San, my wife." I said, still in disbelief that she was really with me.

"MiMi, this is my friend Manu from Spain. I met him in the Valley of Comfort. He travels with us."

MiMi smiled and bowed with respect.

Manu put the tent up and we sat facing our welcome fire, while MiMi cooked for Manu, who had not eaten all day.

"How did you manage to bring her with you?"

"I bought her."

"Bought her!" Manu gasped. "But... how can you buy or sell a wife?"

"In this part of the world women are property, like pigs and water buffaloes. The only difference is that if they don't behave well, buffaloes are sold and a wife is burnt. MiMi's husband tried to kill her but she survived. She was returned her to her parents, who accepted what I offered for her."

Manu was still upset and I continued:

"We do not have to agree with the laws and customs of these people, only respect their way of life. There are many things I would like to change, but my mission is to pass on the Ray of Light to those who ask and not get involved in politics."

"She has a beautiful smile," Manu commented.

I got up and put my arms around MiMi's waist. She closed her eyes and I could sense she was as enthralled as I was by the sudden turn in our lives.

Manu discreetly said he would sleep in the open to allow us intimacy. When we retired to the tent, I heard him mumble:

"Illuminated, yet so human."

Making love to MiMi was a totally different experience after seeing the light of Kun Lun. Each night I spent with her took me back to the wonders of the Mountain. And each morning I awoke by her side filled me with a sense of belonging.

MiMi's father was originally from China and the

language of the village she lived in was very close to mine, but she was almost illiterate. To take advantage of our traveling together, and in anticipation of the day we would arrive at Guilin, I started teaching Chinese to MiMi and Manu. Chinese is a language of tones, and one wrong note can change the meaning of a whole phrase. There were times they made such foolish mistakes, that we had to stop the horses, because it was impossible to ride and laugh at the same time.

MiMi's wholehearted giggling touched me deeply. She commented on how strange it was for her to have fun and not be afraid of being misunderstood or beaten afterwards. Her inner scars were healing, but her face bore testimony of the atrocious violence she had survived.

⊣⊱ ⊰⊢

We were close to the Big City when we saw a wagon appear in the horizon. It was fast approaching us in a cloud of dust. As it drove past us, we heard roaring laughter. Then it suddenly stopped, turned around and approached. A black scarf covered the driver's face and Manu's hand instinctively went for the knife on his waist. The man jumped off the wagon, walked around us and started laughing again.

"By Mohammed and all the holy naked saints! I've been told that the world is round, but that it's the size of a pebble!"

He removed his scarf. It was Zeenath, the jolly merchant from Kashmir.

He took one look at me and spoke before I had the opportunity to greet him:

"I see you have been to Kun Lun. I have often thought about you and your Master. Your enlightened eyes make me regret I didn't talk more with the saint I met in Katmandu. I would give you all I have in the wagon if you could tell me what you found there, but you are mute and unable to give me the enlightenment and peace of mind I see you have attained."

I gave Manu a sign not to speak.

I got off my horse, grabbed Zeenath by the arm and told him to come with me to the wagon. Then I started going through the goods he had there and commenting on them. Zeenath watched and listened with his mouth agape until I burst out laughing:

"My dear Zeenath, your offer is very generous but you need not give me all your possessions in exchange for what I have. But we would like to buy some of your provisions if you have any to spare. Shall we camp and spend the evening together? I shall give you what you ask of me."

Zeenath was shaking his head in disbelief while I talked.

We made a fire and all four of us sat to eat. Zeenath asked me to tell him something about Kun Lun. As I advanced with my story, his expression grew somber. At the point of describing the Gate of Guilt and the dreadful ghosts whirling around us, Zeenath broke down and said with his huge body trembling:

"I'm a greedy man and not worthy of the peace you have found. I have gold in the wagon. When I left the village where I met you – when Master Li Wang was recovering from his wound – the same bandits who attacked you tried to rob me too. They were five against one, but, praise Mohammed, I killed one of them and tied the other four to a tree. Tonight I've struggled all evening with myself, trying to keep my secret, but I cannot bear this guilt and shame any longer; the gold in my wagon belongs to Master Li Wang. Scared that I would kill them too, the bandits confessed it was his. My first thought was to go after you and return the gold, but then I thought about my family and how our lives would change if I kept it. I hid it in my wagon and continued my journey. I don't want to live with this burden."

Then he got up, brought the gold, and said:

"Please forgive me and punish me the way you see best."

I looked at Zeenath with compassion and replied:

"Temptation is no stranger to me. You are forgiven, and the years of guilt and shame have been enough punishment. I shall return the gold to where it belongs. If this were my gold I would be glad to let you keep it. But in return, I shall give you the Light, which is worth much more than the gold."

I placed the Ray of Light in his outstretched hand and asked him to pass it on to any woman,

man, or child, who asked for help.

The moment I gave it to Zeenath I noticed mine was still in my hand, brighter than before, and that Manu's Ray also increased in luminosity.

Zeenath departed the following morning, as abruptly as he had arrived, giving thanks to Allah for his enlightened heart.

I realized I had the power to relieve the suffering of the world.

The YEAR of the Horse gave way to the Lamb as we passed through the Big City. The beginning year was auspicious for all things concerning wealth and family life. We stayed a few days in the City so that MiMi could wonder around the bazaars and see the magnificent New Year Parade. While watching her expressions of joy and enthusiasm, I forgot the noise and the dusty surroundings.

We got new provisions to last us until we would reach Guilin. We also exchanged our horses for new ones and bought one for MiMi. She had been riding with Manu, since they were both small and I was quite heavy.

In spite of the ordinary hardships of any long journey, I enjoyed every moment of it. Ni-hau had no need to hunt food; there were plenty of villages on our way and I was grateful I did not have to eat animals. We saw no bandits and traveled safely through the wilderness.

Passing on the Ray of Light made me understand that I was an instrument of Tao. The Light they received was Forgiveness, Love and Hope. Tao worked miracles through me and changed peoples' lives. All that was required of me was to practice the awareness of each moment that I lived. It was my mission. My occasional prayers turned to a constant thanksgiving to Tao. Even when I spoke, my heart was listening.

River Li was bathing in the sun when we arrived at the hills outside Guilin. We got off our horses to admire the view and Manu stared, out of breath. He said he had seen Chinese paintings with rivers, valleys, pagodas, and cherry trees surrounded by misty hills, but that the scenery before him was far more beautiful than he had imagined. Then he added that he was glad we had finally reached our destination and the long journey had ended, but that he felt insecure about his role after our arrival. He knew I possessed nothing, because I was going to give the gold to Jei-ming in spite of the fact that Master Li had told me to keep it in case I returned without him.

Manu expressed his concern and asked me:

"What will happen to me in Guilin? You have a wife to take care of you, so you don't need me anymore. Where will I go?"

"Do not let your fears of the future spoil this wonderful moment," I said. "Look how the river flows so peacefully, gleaming in the sun. We don't see where it's going, but one day it reaches the sea. In the same way, we do not know what will happen tomorrow. We may take for granted that our tomorrows will be like our yesterdays, but the future is a mystery to all of us. It is very hard to keep that in mind. If we look well to this day, we will see how fragile life is. We will appreciate our loved ones, we find it easier to treat them with kindness, and when they are gone – or when we must leave this world – we will have no regrets."

MiMi looked at the hills captivated and asked:

"Is this beautiful place really your home?"

"It was my home until my Master died. But if you like Guilin, we shall stay in Guilin."

We rode in silence to Master Li's house.

When we arrived at the front door, Jei-ming opened the door and cried out with joy:

"Yu!" I am so glad to see you my old friend!"

Then he swallowed and lowered his eyes.

"My uncle is not with you. Is he arriving later or…?"

"He is with TaiTai," I replied and embraced him. "I will tell you all about it later. This is my wife MiMi San and my friend Manu."

After a long hot bath and a tasty dinner, I told Jei-ming all about our journey. When I finished, he took me to Master Li's garden and said:

"I have done nothing but feed the fish and water the plants, just as my uncle instructed. But look what has happened! The birds must have carried seeds into the garden, now there are more flowers than ever."

I also noticed there were two cherry trees instead of one.

Jei-ming crossed the wooden bridge over the pond and took out a roll of paper from a small hole on the other side.

"Before my uncle left he read this out loud, put it in the hole, and asked me to give it to you in case he would not return."

Jei-ming handed me the scroll and walked away.

I sat down, opened it, and read:

'Dearest Yu,
Rarely have I found it difficult to express my thoughts in an eloquent manner, but the pupil becomes a master and the master turns into a pupil.

Now I find no words to express the gratitude I feel towards you, so I shall be brief: I have given orders to transfer this mansion on your name in case you return without me. This letter in your hand means I am no longer by your side and your mission is over. You may open the doors of this house to anyone you wish, but please do not reveal the secret sign of the garden to anyone.

You have been my servant, my companion and my teacher, but most of all you have been the son I never had. I pray you will be happy here.

Until our paths cross again, I am with you in spirit.

Li Wang'

My tears fell on his words as I bowed to the garden.

EPILOGUE

Master Yu stepped into the beautiful garden of his house that Manu had been tending to so masterfully, and a dog with amber eyes followed him. The sun was shining through the glass roof and two cherry trees were blooming. Little birds were resting their wings on the branches of a square bamboo tree above the pond. Master filled a marble bowl with seeds and the birds chirped joyfully. He sat down on a flat rock and closed his eyes.

The Ray of Light in his hand had grown one hundred fold.

Light steps and the opening of a wooden door interrupted his prayers. It was his two-year old son Yang, who entered hand in hand with his inseparable twin sister Yin. They sat down next to him and he felt happy. Yang's eyes wandered around the garden and he smiled. Suddenly, to Master Yu's great awe, Yang turned to him, put his palms together, crossed the middle fingers and moved them like wings of a little bird.

Master Li and TaiTai had come back.

Made in the USA
Middletown, DE
14 January 2023

21342833R00106